Holy hell, if this was how it felt to kiss a friend, Tommy should have done it years ago. Grayson leaned forward, deepening the kiss, winding his fingers through Tommy's hair. The lap of the water and the calls of the birds all fell away as the pounding of his heart in his ears grew to a crescendo. Grayson guided him, turning him fully, pulling Tommy close, devouring his lips, sending enough heat racing through Tommy to scorch the dock below them.

Tommy pulled back. He had to see Grayson, who cupped his cheeks, holding him still, not letting Tommy get away. He inhaled deeply, struggling for air. "Oh God," Tommy gasped under his breath.

"Is that good or bad?" Grayson asked.

"Do you really have to ask?"

WELCOME TO

DREAMSPUN DESIRES

Dear Reader,

Love is the dream. It dazzles us, makes us stronger, and brings us to our knees. Dreamspun Desires tell stories of love featuring your favorite heartwarming heroes, captivating plots, and exotic locations. Stories that make your breath catch and your imagination soar.

In the pages of these wonderful love stories, readers can escape to a world where love conquers all, the tenderness of a first kiss sweeps you away, and your heart pounds at the sight of the one you love.

When you put it all together, you find romance in its truest form.

Love always finds a way.

Elizabeth North

Executive Director
Dreamspinner Press

Andrew Grey

THE BEST WORST
HONEYMOON EVER

PUBLISHED BY

Published by
DREAMSPINNER PRESS

5032 Capital Circle SW, Suite 2, PMB# 279,
Tallahassee, FL 32305-7886 USA
www.dreamspinnerpress.com

The Best Worst Honeymoon Ever
© 2018 Andrew Grey.

Cover Art
© 2018 Bree Archer.
http://www.breearcher.com
Cover content is for illustrative purposes only and any person depicted
on the cover is a model.

Mass Market Paperback ISBN: 978-1-64108-005-7
Digital ISBN: 978-1-64080-110-3
Library of Congress Control Number: 2017912390
Mass Market Paperback published June 2018
v. 1.0

Printed in the United States of America
∞
This paper meets the requirements of
ANSI/NISO Z39.48-1992 (Permanence of Paper).

ANDREW GREY grew up in western Michigan with a father who loved to tell stories and a mother who loved to read them. Since then he has lived all over the country and traveled throughout the world. He has a master's degree from the University of Wisconsin-Milwaukee and now works full-time on his writing. Andrew received the RWA Centennial Award in 2017. His hobbies include collecting antiques, gardening, and leaving his dirty dishes anywhere but in the sink (particularly when writing). He considers himself blessed with an accepting family, fantastic friends, and the world's most supportive and loving husband. Andrew currently lives in beautiful historic Carlisle, Pennsylvania.

Email: andrewgrey@comcast.net
Website: www.andrewgreybooks.com

By Andrew Grey

DREAMSPUN DESIRES
#4 – The Lone Rancher
#28 – Poppy's Secret
#60 – The Best Worst Honeymoon Ever

Published by **DREAMSPINNER PRESS**
www.dreamspinnerpress.com

To Lynn and Elizabeth. This story is for you!

Chapter One

"YOU'RE going to wear a hole in the floor if you don't stop that pacing," Grayson said with a dramatic eye roll. "You've been doing that for the past hour. Everything is going to be fine."

"Yeah, Uncle Tommy, just chillax," Petey said from where he sat on one of the wooden chairs, legs dangling as he stared intently at the iPhone Grayson had given him to keep him amused.

Tommy Gordon's collar suddenly seemed way too tight, but he didn't pull on it or he'd mess up his bow tie for the millionth time. He had no idea why he was so damn nervous. It seemed like a perpetual state with him, and he hated it most of the time. "Yeah. What business do I have being nervous? It's only my wedding day, and I'm scared to death that I'm going to forget my vows and stand up there, mouth open like some bigmouth bass, and not be able to say a thing."

Tommy began to recite the vows that Petey and Grayson had helped him memorize. Tommy hadn't wanted to use cards during the ceremony, so he'd written his vows out and then rehearsed them so he wouldn't forget. But now his head was a complete blank and he didn't know what he was going to do.

Petey set down his game and slipped off the chair. "Xavier, my heart came alive when I met you, and I hope I make you as happy as you've made me," Petey said, then paused, looking at Grayson. "You know, these vows are kind of sappy."

Grayson swooped in, snatching Petey off his feet. "It's Uncle Tommy's wedding day, and it's the one day when everyone is allowed to be sappy. Especially the guy getting married. So go give him a hug. He really needs one." Grayson held his son in his arms, swinging him back and forth to the music of boyish giggles and happiness before setting him down.

Petey raced over to him, and Tommy accepted the hug and soaked in some of the innocent joy, lightening his worries. This was his wedding day, and he was marrying the man he loved. If he messed something up, so what? They'd continue with the ceremony. They'd still be married and just as happy. Then he and Xavier could start their life together.

"I love you, Uncle Tommy," Petey said when Tommy was about to release him, and he hugged Petey once again.

"I love you too, you little monster." He smiled, and Petey made Godzilla sounds. Tommy laughed, actually laughed, and his nerves receded. This was their day, and he had plenty of backup. Grayson had been the one person to have his back... always, and that wasn't likely to change even now. He set Petey back down, and Petey returned to his video game. "What time is it?"

"There's still half an hour before the start of the ceremony." Grayson shook his head. "You insisted that we get here a full hour early."

"I wanted to make sure everything was perfect," Tommy explained.

Grayson walked across the stone floor of what was usually the bride's dressing room and placed a hand firmly on his shoulder. "How could it not? You planned this down to the smallest detail." He opened his jacket and pulled out a slip of paper. "You put together minute-by-minute cheat sheets for everyone involved so they'd know where they were supposed to be and what they were supposed to do each second of the day. Including reminders not to wear boxers, though I don't know why."

"No one wants to see anything flopping...."

"What would be floppy?" Petey asked.

"Nothing," Grayson told Petey, then pivoted, giving Tommy a stern look, which Tommy returned. "What?"

"You're the only one who got that note," Tommy said and turned away, blowing out his breath in an effort to try to clear his head. This was his wedding day, and he was not going to spend part of it talking about his best friend's junk.

Tommy had never been the kind of guy who was into physical exercise. He was a geek of the highest order. An obsessive geek, if what everyone told him— on a constant basis—was true, and he had little reason to doubt they were right. The proof was being put back into Grayson's jacket pocket, after all. Still, Grayson had convinced him to join the health club with him, and they worked out together three days a week. So needless to say, Tommy had seen what Grayson was packing, though it had taken a little while to get used to seeing guys he knew naked like that.

"Should I be honored, then?" Grayson quipped with a smug grin on his lips.

"Stop it. You're making me nervous again." Tommy began pacing once more. "Can you find out if Xavier is here yet?"

"Did you make up one of these sheets for him too?" Grayson patted his pocket, and Tommy scowled.

"Yes. You know he has trouble getting anywhere on time unless I'm there with him, and we decided he was going to stay with Gary for a few days to make the wedding and the wedding night special." Yeah, he realized now that wasn't one of his brighter ideas. Xavier and Gary had spent that time going out so Xavier could let loose and have some fun. At least that's what he'd been told when he'd texted Xavier to make sure everything was going okay and to tell him he missed him. Apparently Xavier had used those days as a sort of bachelor party.

"You're so old-fashioned," Grayson told him.

"I wanted to do this right," Tommy said softly as the butterflies in his belly finally stopped beating their wings like crazy. He took a deep breath and settled into one of the chairs. "I only plan on getting married once, and I really just want this to be special, for him and for me." The truth was that Tommy was going overboard in order to make sure this was the wedding of a lifetime for Xavier. Tommy knew he was geeky and kind of nerdy—okay, a hell of a lot nerdy—so he'd gone all out to show Xavier that he loved him so he'd be happy with a geek.

"It definitely will be. So just relax while I go check on your husband-to-be." Grayson smiled and left the room, closing the door behind him.

Petey continued playing his game, making occasional faces and laughing.

Tommy sat down next to him. "I like that game too. It's a lot of fun."

"Yeah, but it gets too slow sometimes." Petey fed a dragon a potion, and he smiled and flew away, leaving behind a pile of gold coins that Petey's character scooped up and added to his bag. Petey looked up from the game.

"For you it may be, but there is a lot more to it than just the dragons," Tommy explained.

"I know. But I like the dragons. They're funny, and sometimes when they drink too much berry juice, they fly in circles like they're drunk. That's really funny." Petey laughed and located one of the dragons still on its nest, but he didn't have any berry juice, so he went in search of a patch. That hadn't been what Tommy had had in mind when he'd designed and developed the game, but that was part of the beauty of *Dragons of Archine*. The game could be different things to different players and everyone had fun.

Petey was occupied again, the game drawing him in, and Tommy stood once more, telling himself he wasn't going to pace the room.

"I saw Xavier," Grayson said when he came back inside. "He was heading to his changing room and said he'd be ready."

"He wasn't dressed yet?" Tommy asked, his heart rate shooting up.

"No. Gary was with him. Don't worry. The ceremony is in twenty minutes, and it doesn't take that long to put clothes on."

"How did he look?"

Grayson swallowed and sat down next to Petey, peering over his shoulder for a few seconds. "Why don't you put that down and go to the bathroom so you don't have to during the service. We're going to get started in a little while, and you need to be ready like you promised Uncle Tommy you'd be."

Petey handed his dad back the phone and slid off the chair to hurry to the door. "I'll be right back so you won't be nervous anymore." He pulled the heavy wooden door open and slipped out, closing it with a bang.

"He's amazing," Tommy said, forgetting his nerves for a few seconds. "I'll always remember the first time he called me Uncle Tommy." He reached into his pocket and pulled out a handkerchief to blot his eyes. God, this was more nerve-racking than releasing his first video game to the world.

"Tommy," Grayson said, "I didn't want to say anything in front of Petey, but Xavier looked like hell. My guess is that he stayed out all night and hasn't been home at all. He is changing and getting ready, but God knows what shape he's going to be in. Gary doesn't look like he's in any better shape, and I swear…."

A hesitant knock echoed in the room.

Tommy took a deep breath and went to the door. Grayson stopped him and pointed to one of the chairs. Tommy sat down, trying not to hyperventilate.

"Xavier, what are you doing?"

"I need to talk to Tommy," Xavier said, sounding like shit.

Grayson turned to him, and Tommy lifted his gaze, nodding. Clearly there was something wrong and he needed to deal with it. Whatever plans he'd made were most likely out the window anyway. He certainly hadn't envisioned a drunk, hung-over groom.

Grayson stepped back, pulling open the door, and Xavier half stumbled in, looking worse than Tommy could ever have imagined.

"What the heck happened?" He hurried over, but Xavier stopped him by putting up his hand. "Are you sick?"

"I'm fine," Xavier managed to say, slowly sitting himself down. "Gary and I went out as sort of a last hurrah, and we overdid it." He raised his face, and Tommy got a good look at his glassy eyes.

"Okay. We still have time. Grayson and I can help you get ready," Tommy said gently.

Xavier shook his head of thick black hair, and then his deep brown eyes cleared of some of their rumminess. "I can't do this. The wedding and everything that you've got planned. It's too much." Xavier sat back as all the oxygen seemed to leave the room. Tommy's head grew light, and fuck it all, he was going to faint, but Grayson was there, holding his arm. "You want more than I think I can give."

"You waited to tell him now, twenty minutes before the wedding?" Grayson yelled. "You bastard!"

"I've spent the last few days trying to think about what I was going to do." Xavier hiccupped, and his alcohol breath was enough to knock over an elephant. "I thought if I drank and told myself that I loved you and that I really wanted to do this, everything would be all right. But it isn't true, and I can't go through with this." Xavier got to his feet, half stumbled toward the door, and pulled it open. "I'll see you around." He left and closed the door with a click after him.

Tommy watched, openmouthed, too stunned to move. The room had turned bone-chillingly cold. "What did he just tell me? That he didn't love me?" He couldn't feel his fingers, and then his hands and feet went numb. He tried to think of what he was going to do, but nothing at all came to mind.

"Uncle Tommy," Petey called as he raced into the room, practically barreling into him. "I saw Uncle Xavier and he looked sick. What's wrong?" Petey looked at him and then turned to Grayson.

"Uncle Tommy isn't going to get married. Xavier chickened out and wasn't man enough to tell Uncle Tommy until right now." The anger in Grayson's voice simmered just below the surface. "What he really needs is a hug."

Petey climbed up on the chair, stood up, and hugged Tommy, and Tommy closed his eyes, willing the rest of the world to go away.

A knock on the door caught his attention, and Grayson peered out before opening it for Tommy's mom and dad to come inside. "Things were getting late and no one was ready, so I thought…."

"Oh God, Mom…." Tommy gasped. "He left me."

His mother hurried over, and soon he was hugged by both of them.

"That son of a bitch. I'll string him up by his greasy balls." That was his dad, rough as all hell around the edges, and Tommy had never been so grateful for it in his life.

"He's already gone," Tommy said.

"Son, do you want me to go out there and explain to everyone what's going on?"

"No, I will." Thank God he had decided to keep the ceremony rather small, with only a few dozen people in the chapel. At least it wasn't one of those huge affairs where he'd have to go up in front of half the western world to give an explanation.

"Sweetheart, you don't have to. Everyone will understand."

"No." Tommy hugged his mom and Petey before standing up as tall as his five-foot-nine-inch frame would allow. If anyone was going to do this, it was going to be him. "I need to do it."

"Fine, but we're coming with you." His mother took one of his hands, and Petey took the other. They left the room and went down the short hallway to the chapel that Tommy had had decorated with tons of sprays of every white flower he could find. For a second he took in the scene: the flowers against the gray stone of the chapel, the vaulted timbered ceiling, the small group of people, his friends, coworkers, and extended family, all turning their heads as he entered.

Tommy walked right to the front, where he met the officiant and thanked him softly, then shook his head before turning to those assembled. "I'm sorry, everyone. But there isn't going to be a wedding today. It seems…." Tommy's voice faltered.

"The other groom has left, and Tommy and Xavier will not be getting married."

Thank God for Grayson.

"Tommy would be very pleased if you would all join him for the wedding dinner. I think your support and love are what's going to get him through this difficult time." Grayson put an arm around him, and Tommy wished he hadn't come out here. The looks of sympathy and pity were almost more than he could take. Tommy wanted to hide. Damn, all he needed was to go home, go to bed, and curl up under the covers and not show himself for a week or more.

"Uncle Tommy," Petey said, tugging on his hand. "Can I take this tuxedo off now?"

"Yes," Tommy answered. "Let's go back to the room, and we can all change into more comfortable clothes." He so wanted to get out of his pants and the white afternoon coat. Hell, he never wanted to look at another piece for formalwear again as long as he lived.

People stood, some milling back toward the rear and others coming toward him. He noticed that Xavier's parents were gone, likely when he'd skipped out. That was probably a good thing.

"I'm so sorry," Aunt Virginia said, hugging him tight. "Is it okay to say that I never liked him and that you can do so much better?" She cradled his head, and her warmth and light perfume carried him back to when he was a kid. Aunt Ginny was an amazing woman, independent and self-sufficient, who had never married, and she could be hell on wheels when she wanted to be.

"You can say whatever you want." He was just so happy his family was already circling the wagons. When Aunt Ginny released him, Tommy saw his dad at the back of the chapel, talking softly, a fierce papa-bear expression on his face. If Tommy knew his dad, he was making sure everyone knew this was all Xavier's fault. "But you really didn't like him?"

"No. He was a jerk and spent way too much time worrying about himself." She stepped back and lowered her head in that way she had of looking over her glasses when she was being deadly serious. "He didn't look at you the way he should have, as if you were the beginning and end of his world. He was nice and said the right things, but I never saw the adoration in his eyes that you deserve." She patted him on the shoulder and then drew close once again. "All right, I have to ask you some questions." Just like that she had switched from aunt to family lawyer and all-around advice giver. "Did you follow what I told you?"

"About what?" Tommy was trying to keep up, but his brain seemed like it was in neutral.

"You didn't add his name to your house, did you?"

Tommy shook his head. "You said that being married would handle that, so I didn't do anything."

"How about credit cards or bank accounts?"

"Bank accounts, no. You said that could wait until after the wedding and it would be easier."

"What about credit cards?" She had that look, and Tommy cringed. "Give them to me right now." She held out her hand, and Tommy handed her his wallet. She guided him back into the changing room where he'd been earlier. Petey was in dress pants and a nice shirt, looking much happier as he played his game. Grayson had changed as well. "Which ones?" Aunt Gin asked, holding his wallet open.

Tommy forced himself to concentrate and pulled out the three accounts he'd given Xavier cards for. She took them and asked for his phone, which sat on a tray on the sideboard. Tommy hadn't wanted to carry it during the ceremony. She was already dialing as she crossed to the other side of the room.

"What's going on?" Grayson asked.

"I'm saving this sweet one from financial ruin." Aunt Ginny began punching in numbers, grumbling about getting a live operator.

Tommy turned away. There was only so much he could deal with at the moment. "She's getting Xavier off my credit cards."

Grayson groaned. "It wouldn't surprise me if he tried to buy a damn car on them." His eyes grew hard as rocks. "He wasn't good enough for you."

"Did everyone hate him and not tell me?" Tommy asked, loosening his tie and collar.

"He was a douche," Grayson said vehemently. "Is there anything else that has his name on it?"

Tommy tried to think. "I got him a car as a wedding present. It was delivered today. I meant it as a surprise, but...."

"You bought that in your name, right?"

Grayson was looking out for him. His aunt was doing the same, and so were his folks. Tommy guessed you found out who your real friends and family were when you got jilted at the altar. God, how in the hell was he ever going to get over this?

"I guess so. I mean, I didn't do anything special, so it would have to be. They said I could give it to him later, and we were going to be married, so I figured it didn't matter." He sat down, and Grayson took the suit jacket and handed him the bag of the clothes he'd brought to change into at the end of the reception.

"Get out of those, and I'll put them with mine and return them to the rental place. You might as well be comfortable." Grayson sat between him and Petey.

Tommy sat still, staring at the gray limestone walls, wishing he could just let them swallow him whole. That would be the ticket. If he could simply disappear, then all of this would go away and he wouldn't be the most pathetic man in all of Bayside, Wisconsin. Hell, he could see bus tours driving past his house, making a special trip just to point out the biggest loser on the north shore. *"Here on the left is the home of Tommy Gordon, whose husband-to-be left him at the altar on his wedding day, and on your right is a fine example of prairie-style architecture, circa 1927. It's good to note that no one living there was ever left standing alone on their wedding day. That would be Mr. Gordon, and look, there he is, gardening in his underwear."*

"Tommy." Aunt Ginny's voice pulled him out of his ridiculous daydream. "I need you on the phone."

She patted his shoulder, and he took the phone to answer the questions for the operator.

"I don't show any recent charges," she told him. "If you hold, I'll go ahead and cancel that card for you." Hold music played and then she was back. "That card is canceled, and the only one I have active on the account is the one ending in 3838."

"Thank you. That's my card, so we're good. I appreciate your help."

He hung up, and Aunt Ginny took the phone again and began making another call. He went through the process a second time, and then got on the third call. He explained that he wanted to cancel the card for Xavier Mendota.

"Of course, sir," she said. "I see a number of charges on that account, both last night and up till an hour ago." She rattled off the amounts, and Tommy wondered just what Xavier had been up to last night.

"Go ahead and cancel the card, and then we can review the charges. My attorney will handle things from here." He handed the phone to his aunt, and she answered more questions.

"No. Do not authorize that," Aunt Ginny said.

Tommy got to his feet and went behind the chintz screen to change clothes. By the time he was done, and feeling much better, Aunt Ginny hurried over.

"The bastard just tried to charge a ten-thousand-dollar watch. That was declined," she mouthed and returned to the call. "Thank you. It's canceled? … Wonderful. Can you cancel the other card on the account and reissue a new one in case it's been compromised?" She talked a few minutes longer and ended the call.

"How bad is it?"

"The last few days, about three grand. I stopped the ten-grand purchase, but he'd already charged a little over five thousand and change this morning. There isn't much we can do about those since he had authorization, but he's cut off now." Aunt Ginny turned as Tommy's mom and dad came in. "Rita, honey," she said to his mom. "On your way to the restaurant, stop by Tommy's and make sure jerkwad isn't at the house." She turned back to Tommy. "Call the security company and change all the codes so he can't get in. He's already tried to steal from you, and if he gets into the house, he could damage things or get access to your computer."

Tommy nodded. This was a total nightmare.

"We're on our way," his dad said, squeezing Tommy's shoulder as he walked by.

Tommy called the security company, gave them the vocal codes, and then did what he had to in order to change all the passwords and alarm set codes. Once that was done, he called his dad so he could get inside, then hung up.

"Can I just go home now?" Suddenly the thought of dealing with everyone at a public restaurant was too damn much.

"Of course. Petey and I will take you," Grayson said, and Tommy sat down once again. He was so drained, it was hard for him to stand.

"I'll see to things at the restaurant," Aunt Ginny told him. "Just relax. I doubt anyone is going to expect you to make an appearance." She pulled him into another hug. "If I get my hands on him, I'll castrate the bastard."

Tommy chuckled. God, there were so many reasons why he loved her. "He's not worth it." He held her close for a while, just relishing the comfort, before stepping back. "I'll call you tomorrow."

"You do that. If he shows up and starts causing you any trouble, I can get a restraining order." She grinned and left the room, her violet dress fluttering in her own breeze.

Tommy looked around, making sure there wasn't anything he'd forgotten.

"I talked to the officiant, and he'll lock up and take care of things here. We can go now." Grayson led him outside and to the limousine that Tommy had rented for after the ceremony. Tommy collapsed back in the seat, closing his eyes, wishing this day would just come to an end. Thankfully, Grayson got him inside and explained to the driver the change of plans, and then the car glided away.

"Daddy, look, there's drinks and everything," Petey said.

"Go ahead and open the champagne," Tommy said without cracking his eyes open. "I already paid for it, so we might as well have whatever we like. Petey, you can help yourself to the soda, just be careful." He paid little attention to anything, but smiled at Petey's laughter.

Grayson pressed a glass into his hand, and Tommy took a sip, then emptied the glass and held it out for more. He needed a drink—more than one, as a matter of fact—and at the moment, getting sloshed on bubbly sounded like the best idea of the day.

By the time they turned into the drive and pulled to a stop, Tommy had downed four glasses and was feeling more than a little tipsy as he got out of the car. He had to think of the codes to deactivate the alarm, but it wasn't on.

"Tommy, are you okay, son?" his dad asked almost as soon as he stepped inside.

"He drank half a bottle of champagne in the car so he's not feeling any pain at the moment."

Tommy hugged his dad. "I'm fine, and don't let Grayson exaggerate. Go on and get yourself something to eat. I'm going to sit here, watch some awful television, and then go up to bed and probably stay there for at least two days." He hoped to hell everyone left him alone.

"Can I go play games on the big TV?" Petey asked.

"Sure, bud. Go on and have fun." Tommy wasn't in the mood to make anyone unhappy for any reason. He was already miserable enough for the entire damn world. He flopped down on his leather sofa in the massive living room, turned on the television, and looked through the screen at nothing at all. At the moment, nothing was going to cut through his misery.

"Are you sure?" his dad asked.

"Yeah. You and Mom have a good time and eat plenty. I ordered you the steak because I know you love it." Tommy looked around. "Where is Mom?"

"Where do you think?"

Tommy groaned. "God. Please don't let her cook anything. Not today." His mother was many things, but her cooking was wildly experimental, and usually what came out of her kitchen was good for one and only one thing: the landfill. So many animals had given up their lives for her cooking over the years, Sarah McLachlan would probably ban his mother if she could. Either that or try to bribe her into veganism.

"I'm just making sure you have something to eat that isn't chips or cookies," his mom said, coming into the room and joining his father. "Are you sure you're okay?"

"I'll be fine, Mom. All I want is to be left alone so I can cry like an eight-year-old where no one can see me." Tommy was trying to be lighthearted but knew it fell flat. "Just go and have some fun, eat lots, and for God's sake, make sure everyone has a good time."

"If you say so, dear." She patted his cheek, and Tommy hugged both of them before getting them out the door. As soon as he closed it, he heard the beeps and squawks of the game in the other room.

"You should go and have dinner with everyone else," Tommy told Grayson.

"Petey is having the time of his life. He loves your television. That thing is so massive, he thinks he's getting lost in the game. If you want to go on up and lie down, I'll stay down here with him."

"Whatever you want. Eat anything in the refrigerator. Not that there's very much. I suppose I'll need to get food now." Tommy's head throbbed. "I was supposed to leave on my honeymoon in four days, so there isn't much, but help yourself to whatever there is."

"What are you going to do?" Grayson asked.

"About what?"

"Your trip," he answered, stepping closer.

"I'll probably cancel everything and just stay home. I can work and try to take my mind off this whole awful mess."

Grayson shook his head. "You should go anyway. Why let him ruin a perfectly good vacation? It's been too long since you took some time away, and it would let you get out of town and away from anyone who knows about what happened."

Tommy's shoulders slumped even further. He wasn't sure if he was up for anything at all. The thought of crawling into a cave to hide was overwhelmingly inviting. "I sure as hell don't want to spend an entire week alone." He leaned forward, leveraging himself to his feet. "I can cancel most of the plans and take the hit on the others." Tommy shuffled toward the stairs, almost too tired—and maybe a little drunker than he thought—to lift his feet. "Unless you and Petey want to come."

"He has school, and…."

Tommy looked over his shoulder. "I could say the same thing to you that you just did to me. You don't take vacations either, and I have everything paid for. I could check into having Xavier's ticket transferred or see if there are others available. I have a suite at the resort, so there's plenty of room." He yawned. "Think about it."

He climbed the stairs, went right to his bedroom, and closed the door. He stripped off his clothes and got into bed, pulling the covers over his head. Then and only then did he let his emotions loose and cry the way he'd wanted to for hours.

Chapter Two

GRAYSON Phillips let Petey play on Tommy's superhuge, awesome game system for a while, then figured it was time to go. "Bud, we need to get ready to go home. Uncle Tommy is asleep, and you and I need to leave him alone for a while."

"Dad," Petey said in that tone that crawled up his spine.

"No whining. It's been a really tough day for him." He had to be firm. At nine, Petey was at that age where he pushed boundaries all the time.

"But what if he needs us and we aren't here to help?" Petey asked.

Grayson was pretty sure that was a ploy to play on Uncle Tommy's game system some more, but the way Petey bit his lower lip spoke of genuine concern. "Okay. But put away the games. I think it's time we did something else."

"Can I go swimming?"

"You don't have a suit." Plus, Grayson wasn't planning to stay the rest of the evening.

"Yes, I do. There's one in the bedroom upstairs. I left it here the last time I stayed with Uncle Tommy when you were on that business trip.... Remember? I'll go get it." Petey had the game and television turned off and was out of his seat before Grayson knew what was happening.

"Fine, but be quiet."

Petey was up the stairs in a flash and returned carrying his suit. Normally early April in Wisconsin was way too cold for swimming, but when Tommy had bought the house, it had come with a pool with a pavilion over it, so the pool could be used year-round. Funny, considering that Tommy wasn't a water person... *at all*. In fact, he'd only seen Tommy get in the pool a few times, and that had been because Petey had asked. Even then, Tommy had stayed in the shallow end to play with Petey.

"Come on, Dad." Petey tugged on Grayson's hand, leading him through the house and down the enclosed walk to the pool pavilion. Petey turned on the lights and disappeared into the bathroom to change, then reappeared a few minutes later and jumped into the water, laughing and splashing.

Grayson sat in one of the loungers, watching as Petey played. "I got an email from your mom," he said as he checked his phone.

He'd met Anne in college, toward the very end of his denial phase. God, when he looked back, he realized how stupid he'd been. Years of ignoring who he was, sleeping with as many women as he could just to cover up for the fact that he was gay. He's made many mistakes in his life, but the one with Anne had been his biggest, yet somehow it had turned out for the best.

"Where is she?"

"Zimbabwe. She says she's helping them identify crops they can grow in their climate." Anne sounded amazingly happy, and the pictures of her surrounded by the entire village were incredible.

Petey climbed out of the pool. "Am I going to live with her when she gets back?" He shivered as he dripped on the sand-colored, coated floor.

"No. Your mother and I have come to an agreement. When she gets back, you and she will spend a few weeks together. She wants to travel with you, but then you'll come home and live with me permanently." For too long they had had a shared custody arrangement of sorts, and it wasn't working for Petey. He needed stability, and thankfully Anne was able to see that as well.

"But doesn't she love me?"

Grayson smiled and cradled Petey's cheeks in his hands. "Of course she does. But your mom is one of those people who can never seem to stay in one place for very long. She needs Africa and a bunch of places all over the world. You need school and friends and…." Grayson swallowed. "I need you with me." That was the truest thing he had ever spoken. He hadn't expected to be a father, and he hadn't known he had become one until Petey was two and a half. Then Anne had contacted him, and after some hurt feelings, they'd worked things out. Now he couldn't imagine a life without Petey in it. "Go on and swim."

Petey raced back to the water, and Grayson smiled at his exuberance.

"I thought he'd get you out here at some point," Tommy said as he came in, sitting in the lounger next to Grayson's. Tommy looked like hammered shit, to be blunt. His hair pointed in all directions, and he had light circles under his eyes, his lips drawn downward, and no energy whatsoever.

"Did you sleep?"

"Yes and no. I might have dozed off, but then Xavier was there to tell me how much he didn't love me once again, and I kept playing things over and over in my head." Tommy sat back. "You know…."

"What?" Grayson prompted, knowing he needed to let Tommy talk.

"This whole thing sucks." Tommy closed his eyes, and Grayson sat back. He didn't know what to say and figured keeping quiet was the best thing to do. "Will you and Petey come with me?"

Grayson thought about it and reached for his phone. He stared at it, then pulled up a number and made a call. "Jan, it's Grayson. I'm sorry to bother you on a weekend, but…." He wasn't sure how to bring this up.

"Aren't you supposed to be at a wedding?" Jan was an amazing supervisor and one of the best people he'd ever met. They were friends of a sort and had worked together since Jan hired him out of college. Jan had promoted Grayson to a project manager a few years earlier, pleased with his work. "Yes, I was. But one of the grooms was a no-show, and I'm here with Tommy right now. I know it's short notice, but he's asked me to go with him on a trip, and I have plenty of vacation time…."

Jan chuckled. In the world of computers, Tommy was sort of a local legend. "You go. You're between projects right now. Take the time off. You deserve it." She seemed happy. "So what kind of trip is this?"

"Bonaire," Grayson said, and Petey whooped from where he stood near them.

"That's amazing. I've been there with the boys, and they had the time of their lives." Jan loved to travel, and her sons were huge into scuba diving. There were pictures all over her office. "When do you leave?"

"Wednesday."

"See me first thing on Monday so I'll know your schedule." She ended the call, and Grayson put his phone back in his pocket.

"I get to go too?" Petey asked in that tone that said he was making sure.

"Yes," Tommy answered. "You definitely get to go too. Your dad will have to talk to your teacher, and before you ask, yes… you will have to do homework and probably a report on your trip because you'll be out of school, but you get to go."

Petey whooped again and raced back into the water, then sent up a splash that got both of them sprinkled with spray.

"You made his day."

Tommy rolled his head on the lounge to face Grayson, cracking open his eyes. "Thank you. I'll make all the arrangements for both of you just as soon as I can get out of this chair, and you clear what you need to." Some of the lines around Tommy's mouth smoothed out as he relaxed.

"Can I ask why you, the least water-friendly person I know, would go to Bonaire, a water paradise, on your honeymoon?" Sometimes Tommy's logic completely mystified him.

"Xavier wanted to go there, and I wanted to make him happy. My choice would have been to go to Paris for the week. It's spring, and Paris is supposed to be stunning this time of year. They even write songs about it." Tommy sighed. "But I did what he wanted."

"Why?" Grayson asked softly.

Tommy sat up, his eyes filling and his face contorting in pain. "Because I wanted him to love me. Because I was so desperate to be loved by someone, and not be alone, that I didn't see that Xavier didn't really care and was only interested in me for... what I had." Tommy covered his face, shoulders raising and lowering.

Grayson shifted on the lounge, gathering Tommy in his arms, holding him tightly. "It's all right." He never got much of a chance to hold Tommy, and it felt so good. The truth was that he'd had a kind of crush on him for years, but Grayson hadn't wanted to jeopardize their friendship, and Tommy had never seemed interested in him in that way. A year ago, sometime after his breakup with Jeffrey, Grayson had decided he was going to say something to Tommy, but then Tommy had called to say he'd met the most amazing guy. Tommy and Xavier had dated, then gotten engaged. There was no way Grayson would ever have said anything after that. Tommy had seemed so happy.

It was true that Grayson had hated Xavier, but he'd always thought that was because of his feelings for Tommy. Throughout his and Tommy's relationship, Grayson had kept his feelings quiet because he didn't want to hurt Tommy. Now Xavier was out of the picture in spectacular fashion, but that changed nothing for Grayson. It wasn't like he could confess his feelings now that Tommy was hurting so badly. It seemed the fates had deemed the two of them were to be friends only. Grayson could live with that; he'd have to.

He rocked back and forth, doing his best to comfort Tommy as he dealt with the first waves of grief and loss. "I promise you it will be okay."

"What's wrong with me?" Tommy pulled away, sniffling and wiping his eyes. "I know Xavier had style and was really hot, but why didn't he love me?"

Grayson didn't have an answer right away. "I think in some way he did."

Tommy sniffled again, and Grayson wondered what kind of a fool Xavier was. How anyone could not love Tommy was beyond him. He was kind and generous almost to a fault. Tommy had tons of money and could afford almost anything he wanted in life, but he was the most down-to-earth, gentle man Grayson had ever met. Sure, he had his quirks, but everyone did.

"Yeah, right…." Tommy coughed lightly, probably to clear his throat, and wiped his eyes once again.

Grayson put his hands on each of Tommy's shoulders. "I thought Xavier was a gold digger. I think he stayed with you for the money. But in the end, he couldn't do it." Grayson really thought Xavier was the biggest ass on the face of the earth, with no redeeming qualities at all. But he didn't think that was what Tommy needed to hear. Tommy seemed so fragile that Grayson didn't want to hurt him any more.

"Do you think so?" Tommy's eyes glistened, and he had that kicked-puppy look.

Grayson tried to think. "I don't know what else to say." He sighed. "Look at it this way. He called it off before the wedding. If he had done it afterward, then he'd be stuck in a way, and you'd be much more hurt once he took you for what he could." Grayson didn't want to remind Tommy that Xavier tried to put a ten-thousand-dollar charge on one of his credit cards after he'd broken things off. That was just theft and pure greed. "Has he tried to call?"

Tommy shook his head. "I sort of blocked his number."

Dang, Tommy was thinking more clearly than Grayson thought he had been. "Good for you." He hugged Tommy once again. "Just try not to think about him too much and look forward to the trip. It'll be just the three of us, and we'll have a lot of fun."

Tommy nodded. He didn't seem totally convinced, but at least he wasn't as gloomy as he'd been.

"Uncle Tommy, will you come in the water with me?" Petey asked, leveraging himself up on the side of the pool.

"I don't think so, buddy, not today. But when we're on vacation, I promise I'll go swimming with you." Tommy was trying to paste on a smile, though it really wasn't working. "You have fun, and if you want, look in the pump room. I got some toys and stuff. The only thing is, you can't get your dad and me wet."

"Okay." Petey climbed out, raced to the room, and pulled open the door. Grayson wondered what Tommy had bought because Petey stilled and then let out a whoop that filled the enclosure. He came back with a water gun half as big as he was. "This is awesome."

"Remember not to squirt us," Grayson warned as Petey jumped into the pool to fill it.

"I should have known Xavier was a pile of crap when he and Petey didn't get along." Tommy sighed. "I mean, who doesn't just love a kid like that?"

"He plays well with other kids and he does well on his own." There wasn't much more Grayson could ask for.

He leaned back on his lounger, and they grew quiet, the only sound coming from Petey as he played. Eventually Tommy ordered takeout from Cousin's Subs because they all loved them. They didn't normally deliver, but Tommy was so well-known to the local store and such a good customer, along with being a great tipper, they made an exception. In fact, Grayson had been in the store when Tommy was placing an order, and the employees had argued over who would do the delivery because of the tip.

After half an hour, the doorbell rang. "I'll get it. You get the water baby out of the pool."

The sun had set, and Grayson turned on the pool lights. "Come on, squirt. Let's get out and dried off. We're going to have dinner and then we'll go home."

"Dad...."

"I know you'll stay in the water until you're a complete prune, but we need to give Uncle Tommy some space. Besides, you'll have plenty of time to spend in the water once we go away." Grayson grabbed a towel and wrapped Petey in it once he padded over. "Go on and change, and then you need to put everything away before you come eat."

Petey huffed but did as he was told, and Tommy joined them, the phone at his ear.

"Yeah, this was supposed to be a honeymoon, but I got left at the altar, so I want to change the name on one of the airline tickets and get another seat on the same flights. ... Yes, first class." Tommy grinned briefly. Apparently those were the magic words to get done whatever Tommy wanted. "Yes, the same down and return flights." He spelled out Grayson's name, as well as Petey's. "Great. Thank you so much. ... No, I need to give you a different card. That one was canceled." Tommy seemed to be able to get done what he needed, but as soon as he hung up, he flopped on the lounge like he'd expended all the energy he had. "We're all set. I have your plane tickets, and the rest we can handle when we get there." He shut his eyes, and once Petey had finished changing and put away all the toys, they closed up the pool and went inside the house, pulling the large patio-type doors closed.

EVERYTHING as far as his job, and even with Petey's school, went like clockwork. Grayson had explained the situation to his teacher, Mrs. Guilder, which had resulted in one hilarious phone call about Petey going on a honeymoon, that left them both in stitches. Mrs. Guilder had been concerned about him being gone, but Grayson had promised he'd do all his work. "He'll also put together a presentation that he can share with the class about the ocean life around the island. We'll bring back things you can use." Mrs. Guilder had been thrilled about that, since they were going to be starting a series of lessons on the oceans.

Grayson spoke with Tommy each day, but otherwise he hadn't heard much from him. Apparently he was deep in developing a new project and was working around the clock. Somehow Grayson doubted that Tommy was making any meaningful progress and was only doing what he could to keep himself as busy as hell.

"Are we going now?" Petey had been beside himself for four days and had barely slept since he found out he was going on a honeymoon.

"Yes. Go get your bag and wheel it out to the front door."

Packing with Petey had been a hoot. He'd tried to put half his clothes and his toys into the suitcase. Grayson had worked with him to only pack what he was going to need in his suitcase, and then they'd packed his Star Wars bag for him to carry on the plane.

Grayson followed Petey through the house as he wheeled his bag, carrying the rest, and placed them next to the door. Then he sat Petey in the chair and had him stay there while he checked the house. By the time he returned, Petey had curled up in a ball and was half-asleep. Not that he was surprised. It had been a long day already, they had the drive to Chicago tonight, and their flight left very early in the morning.

Lights flashed outside the house, and Grayson stepped out into the cool night air. Tommy climbed out of the limousine, the driver loaded the bags, and then they got inside. Grayson laid Petey on one of the seats, covered him with a blanket, and then they were off.

"Our flight is first thing in the morning out of Chicago. We have plenty of travel ahead of us." Tommy settled back on the seat, and Grayson did the same thing as the car pulled out of the drive.

TOMMY wasn't kidding. A drive to Chicago, a plane to Charlotte early in the morning, then a flight to Aruba, and hours later they were on a small island-hopper to Bonaire. Thankfully Petey had slept most of the way. "Look at that," Grayson said as they circled over the crescent-shaped main island.

"What's that?" Petey asked.

"Klein Bonaire…. Little Bonaire," Tommy explained. "It's where a lot of the reefs are."

"Can we go swimming out there?" Petey asked, pointing at the open water.

"I think swimming will be in the resort pool, and the other water sports will be out there." Tommy looked out the window. He was still nervous and upset, but he seemed calmer than he'd been.

They landed at the small airport and got their luggage. Then they found the car for the resort and piled in for the short drive to the water's edge.

"Are we staying here?" Petey asked as they got out in front of a stucco main building, with palm trees all around. He stood, looking up and all around him. "This is so cool!"

"Isn't it?" Tommy said, taking Petey's hand. "Come on. Let's go inside." He took Petey in while Grayson handled the luggage and gave one of the porters Tommy's name.

"Yes. We have his room. I take it all there," the handsome man with dark skin and bright eyes said with a smile. Grayson handed him a generous tip, and he got a cart, placing all the luggage on it, and then wheeled it away.

By the time Grayson got inside, Tommy had keys and a bellman was motioning them back outside, this time on the ocean side.

"We are a small island," he said in a heavy Caribbean accent that sounded like music to Grayson's ears. "We have diving, snorkeling, and plenty of chill time. Nothing happens quickly here, and that's exactly the way everyone likes it." He turned to Tommy. "Smile, man, you on vacation!" He grinned again, and dang it if Tommy didn't smile, a genuine smile that reached Grayson's heart. He had wondered if Tommy was ever going to smile again.

"All right," Tommy agreed, and they strolled along a concrete walkway, past various resort buildings, glimpsing the water between them. Tropical breezes wafted through the trees, carrying salt spray and the taste and scent of clean, open water. Grayson could feel the pressures and worries of home slipping away by the second.

"Here is your bungalow," the bellman said. "It has its own dock with its own boat. Just call to the desk and we will have someone available to take you out whenever you wish. There is also a butler who will be at your disposal." He smiled. "We hope you have a good honeymoon."

"No, no," Tommy said, stammering slightly. "My honeymoon fell through. These are my friends, and they came with me." He looked down. "It was pretty awful."

"Then have a good time, and please call if we can be of any service." He unlocked the door and motioned them inside. Their luggage was already waiting for them, and they stepped into a spacious living area with a red tile floor, rich sofas, a bar, kitchenette, and to Grayson's surprise, two bedrooms. The patio doors on the ocean side opened directly onto a deck that connected to their private dock. A small cabin cruiser rocked back and forth in the waves.

"It's perfect."

"Can we go for a boat ride?" Petey asked, racing to the doors.

"Don't go out there," Grayson said, hurrying over as Tommy directed the bellman where to put the luggage. "You have to promise me that you won't go out there without me or Uncle Tommy, okay?"

"But…." Petey gazed longingly at the water.

Grayson opened the door and they walked out. "See, the bottom of the water is all coral and it will cut your feet. This isn't a swimming area, so you have to be careful. So I want you to promise me." He turned Petey, looking into his eyes.

"I promise."

"Not ever…."

"Okay. I'll never come out here unless you or Uncle Tommy is with me." Petey sighed, sounding put upon.

"Do I have to keep the door locked?" Grayson knew he was being stern, but he needed to make sure Petey understood. Petey shook his head slowly, and Grayson led them back inside, closing the door behind them.

"The bags are in the rooms. I think we should change clothes and then try to find something to eat. The resort serves food by the pool, so we can sit, eat, and this one"—

Tommy mussed Petey's hair—"can go swimming. But only after he's eaten."

Petey raced off to the bedroom that he and Grayson were sharing. Grayson followed, knowing if he didn't that all Petey's clothes would get strewn everywhere.

"Your suit is in your Star Wars bag." Grayson helped Petey get it on the bed, and then he opened it and rummaged until he found the suit. Petey hurried to the bathroom, and Grayson found him a T-shirt and some sandals, laying them out. Grayson figured he'd unpack later, so he took his suit out and changed into it, getting ready so they could go right away.

"I'm ready, Dad," Petey pronounced, and Grayson tossed him his shirt and handed Petey the sandals. "Go on out and wait for Uncle Tommy. Then we can go."

Grayson finished getting the things they'd need in a carry bag and joined the others. They left for the pool, stepping outside into a tropical paradise that took Grayson's breath away.

"Bonaire is largely a desert island. They don't get a lot of precipitation, so there isn't dense rain forest. It's more succulents and smaller plants that need less water."

"What's that?" Petey asked, pointing toward the water.

"A mangrove. It's a plant that uses sea water. It's unique that way and can grow right on the beach. They get flowers sometimes and really tangle." Grayson showed Petey, who immediately lost interest as soon as one of the tiny lizards caught his eye, and he raced off after it. "Stay on the path," Grayson told him, and Petey skidded to a stop as a larger iguana stared back at him. "Don't get too close."

"That's cool, Dad. Can I get one of those for a pet?" Petey stared, and the lizard turned and slowly walked away into the tangle.

"No. You can't get every animal you see for a pet," Tommy teased, taking Petey's hand. "Come on. Let's get to the pool so we can eat before we all waste away to nothing." Tommy turned to Grayson, and he saw the first sparkle returning to Tommy's eyes. It was wonderful to see.

They found a table and chairs near the pool under the cabana that housed the bar and a small restaurant. Petey wanted to go swimming, but Tommy wasn't particularly hungry right then, so he and Grayson decided to wait a little to order. Grayson went ahead and got food for Petey and afterward had him sit for a few minutes to let his belly settle. Then he turned him loose after slathering him with sunscreen. He and Tommy perused the menu to decide on their own meals.

"The curry looks interesting," Grayson said. "I understand it's a Caribbean thing and I'm going to try it. You can have some if you like."

"Good. Then I'm going to get the goat and we can share." Tommy closed his menu and placed the orders with the bartender. Grayson read his name badge, Johan, and smiled. It struck him as strange until he remembered that the island was Dutch.

"Are you really going to get in the pool?" Grayson teased. He had to.

"I promised Petey I would, and I keep my promises, unlike some people." Tommy grumbled the last part. "How can someone not know whether they want to get married? I mean, he could have said something a long time ago, but he had to wait until the day of the wedding…." Tommy accepted the tall beer from Johan and downed half of it.

"Slow down." Grayson touched his hand, and a tingle slid up his arm. "I know you're upset, and it's okay when that happens, but don't drink too much. You're going to get in the water, and being drunk or buzzed isn't a good idea."

Tommy set his glass on the bar. "I know that. But...." He sighed and clenched his hands.

"You want to punch the shit out of him, don't you?" Grayson asked, and Tommy smiled.

"I want to string him up by his balls and castrate the bastard. Maybe cover him in honey and put him on a hill of fire ants. Let those bastards have at him for a while." Tommy grinned. "I've had plenty of time to get creative. I thought it would be cool to do the honey thing and then leave him tied to a tree in northern Wisconsin. Let one of the bears they have up there have at him."

"Come on. The poor bears. He's so greasy, the creature would have a heart attack." Grayson figured he'd go for humor, and Tommy chortled. "You could always do better than him." He took Tommy's hand. "Do you remember when we met? I was a senior and you were a freshman at Marquette. I had to pass that dang calculus class so I could get my degree. I do okay in math, but that never made any sense. You were this geeky, tiny—damn it all, I'll say it—cute-as-a-button freshman, and you understood everything the teacher said before he said it."

"And you were struggling, bad."

"So you came up to me and offered some help if I needed it."

Tommy smiled. "And we've been friends ever since."

"Yup. And if Xavier can't understand that you're the kind of guy who would ask someone else if they needed help, then he isn't worth your time or energy. Not for a second." Grayson had always thought Tommy was a man in a class by himself. "You always work hard for everything you have, and you help others along the way." That was the best kind of man Grayson could ever hope to have met, and he'd managed to do it when he was twenty-one. Not that he understood just how special Tommy was at the time. That little seed of knowledge had taken a long while to grow.

But he understood it now, and that was part of the problem. Grayson understood what it was he wanted now. When he'd had his chances, he'd been quiet, too nervous to go after it, and once he'd understood what that was, the opportunity had been gone, the door closed. One thing Grayson knew was that there was no way Tommy was ready to start anything with anyone new, and Grayson wasn't going to be some sort of rebound. His heart couldn't take that, not with Tommy.

Tommy slid off the bar stool and hugged Grayson from behind. "Thanks," he whispered, but he might as well have trapped a bubble of heat around them. Suddenly Grayson was too warm and his heart beat faster. He inhaled the sweet tropical scent, but it was colored with the rich, earthy aroma of a man. Grayson bit his lower lip to stifle a groan as he leaned into the touch, taking what he could get. "You know how to make me feel better."

"Uncle Tommy," Petey said, hurrying over. "Are you going to come in?"

"Yes. As soon as your dad and I eat. I promise." Tommy turned toward the pool. Other kids were playing and having a good time. "Have you made friends?" Petey nodded, and Tommy pulled out his wallet to hand Petey some money. "There's a store right over there. Go see what they have for pool toys and decide what you want." He pressed the bills into Petey's hand. "Have fun."

Petey raced away, came back, thanked Tommy, and hugged him. By the time he actually left, Tommy's shirt had water spots on it and he was smiling even wider.

"You don't need to do that," Grayson said without heat.

"He's as close to a child as I'm ever going to get." The dark shadow that had momentarily shifted away slid back over Tommy's features. "So let me spoil him a little. He's away from home, and I want him to have fun."

"If you want to have some fun," Johan broke in with a wide grin, passing over a laminated sheet, "these are some of the activities the resort offers. I can recommend this one." He pointed to a snorkeling adventure. "It's all afternoon, and they take you out to Klein Bonaire. You drift over the coral, sponges, and everything."

Grayson lifted his gaze to Tommy, who looked less than thrilled.

"It's incredible…. Really."

"Maybe I'll take Petey," Grayson said as he continued looking over the list. "Okay, I like this one. It's a watersports package. A guided snorkel like he described, snuba, whatever that is, an evening sail, and a tube-running excursion." Dang, that all sounded like amazing fun, and Petey would adore it.

Tommy muttered something and turned away.

"What?"

"We already have all that," Tommy said more loudly. "Xavier signed us up for all that, plus an extra snorkeling excursion because he said he loves it. The last one was a special all-day water fun package, with lunch, drinks, and a chance to see some of the island's hidden gems. Since they're all for two, I thought you and Petey could go."

Grayson ground his teeth a little and looked at Johan. "Is it possible to add a third person to our existing reservations? The last name is Gordon." He wasn't going to leave Tommy behind. The purpose of coming here wasn't so Tommy could stew while he and Petey were out having fun.

"Of course," Johan said, reaching for the phone under the bar.

"Come on. You're going to have fun. I know you aren't much of a swimmer, but they have float belts and vests, so all you have to do is enjoy." Grayson pointed to the information on the card. "There's nothing to be worried about."

"Do you want the charges added to the room?" Johan asked.

"Yes," Tommy answered and sighed almost painfully. "I'll see how it goes."

Johan took care of the reservations, then left and returned with their food, which smelled amazing, the scent blending perfectly with the others around him. The curry wasn't hot, but was as flavorful as anything he'd ever had. Grayson realized just how hungry he was when he took his first bite. The chicken was served with fries that tasted heavenly in the curry sauce, and he ate ravenously.

They had intended to share, but Tommy seemed to be doing the same, and their conversation paused while they inhaled their food. Grayson did offer a bite to Tommy, who did the same in return, but mostly they ate and groaned at the amazingness of it all.

"Is everything okay?" Johan asked.

"It's amazing," Grayson said, finishing the last bite.

"And gone," Johan observed.

"Yeah." Grayson used his napkin and thanked Johan as he cleared the plate. Now he felt human again. His belly was full, he was in a tropical paradise, and Petey was laughing and happy in the pool. Everything would be perfect if he could get Tommy to smile. Hell, heaven on earth would be getting Tommy to smile because Grayson had just made his eyes roll to the back of his head. But miracles rarely happen, and he needed to take what he could get.

"Thank you, Johan," Tommy said quietly as Johan took his plate. He was presented with the check, and Tommy signed it to the room with what looked like a generous tip.

"You're welcome. The schedule for your various excursions will be delivered to your room. I think they start Saturday, so you'll have all day tomorrow. There will be a cruise ship in, so go into town." Johan pointed, and they could see the town in the distance. "Local artists will set up a market, and you can get some really fun things other than just touristy T-shirts and stuff if you'd like."

"Sounds good," Tommy said. "Thanks." He slid off the stool and walked to the edge of the shade. The sun was going down and the pool was mostly shadowed by the surrounding buildings. He pulled off his shirt and dropped it on a lounge chair.

"I brought you a towel," Petey said, pointing to a different lounge, and Tommy picked up his shirt to transfer it to the one Petey had chosen.

Grayson smiled. Tommy had always been good with Petey, even when he'd first come to live with him. It had been Tommy who had taken Petey to the playground near their house and got him to go down the slide for the first time. They'd laughed and giggled together, and then Petey had talked Uncle Tommy into going down each slide. After that, there had been no stopping him.

"Come on in!" Petey called, and Grayson watched as Tommy got in the water step by step. He was so pale and looked even more so in his dark blue suit. Grayson didn't mind at all. Tommy wasn't tall, but he was lithe and lean, with ab lines on his belly. Not because he exercised, but because when he was working, he forgot to eat a lot of the time.

Tommy turned toward him, the suit hanging on his hips, and Grayson made a note to get Tommy one that fit when they were in town. Not that he really minded, especially when his imagination traveled down Tommy's chest to his hips and what he was packing below. Grayson knew Tommy's body fairly well. He'd seen him on multiple occasions at the gym, and he definitely had nothing to snicker at. Hell, if Tommy wore clothes that actually fit, everyone would see how hot he was. So... maybe new clothes were a bad idea.

"Dad!"

"I'm coming." Grayson pulled off his shirt and slid into the water. It was the perfect blend of warm and refreshing. Petey swam right over into his arms. Grayson laughed, and Petey stood on his hands to jump off and into the water. "Come on, Tommy. The pool is only five feet at its deepest. There's nothing to worry about."

Tommy stepped off the bottom step, and Petey raced over to him. "Uncle Tommy! We can play catch." He jumped to a nearby ball and threw it to Tommy. Sometimes Petey was brilliant. Tommy began catching and throwing the ball, forgetting he was in the water. He hurried to retrieve it when he missed, and once or twice he even swam.

It seemed that Petey had gotten squirt guns as well, and once those came out, it was a three-way war that left all of them laughing and completely drenched. Tommy's shaggy brown hair ended up plastered to his forehead and in his eyes. He grinned and shot at Petey, who retaliated.

"What do you think of a water fight video game?" Tommy asked, putting down his gun. "I could build different water situations, including lagoons, pools, bays, even fights on rafts. There could even be target-shooting ranges, all with water guns rather than bullets." He hurried over to Petey, lifted him up, and tossed him giggling into the water.

"That would be awesome, Uncle Tommy. Dad won't let me play *Call of Duty* and stuff."

Tommy nodded. "Your dad's right. That's way too violent and old for you. But if I did this right, it could be fun for kids and adults. Just think about it—a game of skill that left your opponents drenched instead of dead. There could even be a water balloon component." Tommy turned and headed for the steps. "I have to write this down before I forget."

"Uncle Tommy!" Petey called.

"He'll be back," Grayson said, turning his water gun onto his son to distract him.

Tommy wasn't gone long, thankfully, and he got back into the water.

"Can you stand on your hands?" Petey asked Tommy, then proceeded to show him how it was done.

"That's awesome, but I'm a little old for that." There was no way Tommy was going to do anything like that. Getting him in the water was enough of a feat for one day.

"Dad can do it." Petey swam over, and Grayson stood on his hands, but ended up flopping down after just a few seconds. Still, he made Petey happy.

"We need to get out in a few minutes, so have your last fun and then we'll get dried off, dressed, and we can walk into town to see about a restaurant for a late dinner." There was some good food on the island according to a number of websites, and Grayson figured they'd eat at the resort plenty.

"Dad," Petey whined, and Grayson gave him the look that said he wasn't going to be pushed.

Petey swam a little while longer and then got out of the water and into a towel. Tommy did the same as Grayson dried himself, then led the pack back to their bungalow.

Grayson got Petey changed, which was a feat. He had so much energy and it was all going in so many directions at the moment. He knew Petey would crash after dinner, but until then he hummed from one thing to the next. By the time they were both dressed, Tommy was waiting for them in the living area. They got their keys and headed out.

The sidewalk in front of the resort led toward the small downtown area. It was quaint, with brightly colored shops, a few with touristy items, and some restaurants that looked like they catered mostly to locals.

As soon as they stepped inside one, the scents that assailed them were out of this world. They took a seat, and a server approached. He explained the menu and brought their drinks.

"I think this could turn out to be exactly what I needed," Tommy said as local musicians filled the space with Caribbean sounds and rhythms. The server brought him a Polar, and Tommy sighed as a few more of the lines around his eyes smoothed out.

"Is this a bar?" Petey asked.

"I think it's a restaurant and a bar. So you need to be on your best behavior and act as grown up as possible." Grayson winked at Tommy and received one in return as a kid two tables over threw a fit of epic proportions. Grayson glanced at Petey to see how he'd react and caught one of his epic eye rolls before he sat up straighter. Grayson gently patted Petey's back and wondered when he was going to insist on being called Pete or Peter. They grew up so fast.

"What are we doing tomorrow?" Petey asked as he pulled the straw out of his soda and drank from the glass.

"Sleeping in. We've been traveling for a long time and we're all tired. Then we'll have a late breakfast, and the man from the resort told us about a market that was being set up because there's a cruise ship coming in, so we'll see that," Tommy explained. "Then you can spend some time at the pool."

"Is that all?" Petey asked.

"For tomorrow. Later this week we have snorkeling for two days, snuba, which I need to figure out, and tube running, as well as an evening on a sailboat. But yes, we could also take the boat out tomorrow if you want."

That more than satisfied Petey, and he went back to his drink. Their server returned, and they ordered fresh seafood appetizers, as well as entrees that would make any seafood restaurant in the States green with envy. And by the time they were done, they rolled themselves out of the restaurant and trudged back to their bungalow, where they nearly fell onto the sofas.

"Go ahead and get ready for bed," Grayson told Petey, who was desperately trying to stay awake. "Everything will be here when you get up, I promise."

Petey hugged Tommy and then went into the bedroom. Grayson put his feet up, relaxing as he watched the light outside the patio doors redden and then fade away altogether. When he didn't hear any more from Petey, he got up and went into the room. Petey was on his bed, lying on his side, the window open, letting in the fresh, slightly cooling sea air. Grayson went over to him and leaned down to stroke Petey's hair lightly before leaving the room once again.

"He's completely out," Grayson said and walked to the sliding doors. Pulling them open, he stepped out onto the dock and walked out toward the boat. He sat, leaning back against one of the pilings, looking upward. Above him, a million stars danced in the night. He'd never seen so many in his life. "Beautiful, isn't it?" he asked when Tommy joined him.

"Yes." Tommy sat next to him, sharing the piling, their shoulders touching. Grayson didn't dare move, not wanting Tommy to pull away. "I'm beginning to think I was a fool."

"Why?" Grayson asked in a whisper. It seemed almost sacrilegious to speak any louder.

"I didn't want to come here. And I would have missed this."

The water lapped gently on the shore and the breeze rustled overhead. A few birds called out, and occasionally something rustled through the plants near the shore. "What's amazing is the lack of sounds of other people." Though Grayson was acutely aware of one particular person and his close proximity. He closed his eyes, inhaling deeply, catching just the slightest scent of sweat and musk from Tommy. God, he loved that scent. Few things were as enticing.

Tommy took a deep breath and sighed. "Do you think I'm desperate?" He shifted slightly before Grayson could answer. "I mean, do you think I wanted a boyfriend so badly that I took the first one to come along and fell in love with him?"

Grayson thought before he spoke. "We don't always have control over what our hearts want. But no. I think you met Xavier and fell in love. It isn't your fault he didn't fall in love back." He paused, wondering how to continue. "I think relationships are a lot like business agreements."

Tommy chuckled.

Grayson raised a hand. "No. Hear me out. See, when you're in one, you give your heart and you expect that the other person is going to be honest in their feelings for you. They don't have to give their heart in return, but they should tell you their true feelings. That's the deal. Xavier should have said a long time ago that he didn't feel the way you did. Yeah, it probably would have hurt, but a lot less than what he did." Grayson shifted and realized that Tommy was leaning forward. He scooted behind him and slowly rubbed his shoulders. "He's the one who dropped the ball and let you down. It isn't the other way around." He increased the pressure, and Tommy let out a little moan. Grayson continued working on Tommy's muscles, loving the feel of them under his hands.

"But I keep wondering why I didn't see it." Tommy leaned forward farther, and Grayson let his hands wander lower, working his back. "God, that's so good."

"Just relax," Grayson breathed just loudly enough to be heard over the lap of the water.

Tommy relaxed under his hands, and it was wonderful to feel. "You always take care of me."

Grayson nodded and continued working the kinks out of Tommy's back. "You didn't see it because he didn't let you see it. Remember, he allowed you to plan the wedding, the honeymoon, and everything for months and said nothing. And he broke it off."

"I know."

"Well, I talked to your aunt the other day, and you need to call her," Grayson said, rubbing a particularly tight spot. "Once we get home."

"Why?" Tommy said.

"Because he owes you for half of all the wedding expenses." Grayson loved the idea of sticking whatever he could to Xavier. The guy deserved it in spades.

"I don't want to draw things out like that. If I do nothing, he's out of my life and I don't have to have anything to do with him or ever see him again, and that's what I want." Tommy sat up straighter, and Grayson got comfortable, letting Tommy lean against him, which was amazing. What surprised Grayson was how natural it felt, and his arms wound themselves around Tommy's waist. He didn't want to go too far, but Tommy settled, and Grayson wasn't going to back away unless Tommy wanted him to.

"Sometimes there's a price to be paid for your actions." Grayson closed his eyes. He wasn't going to push it.

"True, and Xavier will pay that price eventually. The cosmos will find a way of biting him in the ass. But I'm not going to do it. I've cut him off and he can't get to me financially, and Mom and Dad are watching the house, so that's covered. He can do whatever he wants now because I'm out of it."

Grayson hoped that was true.

"Besides, I'm here with you and Petey rather than him." Tommy swept his hand in front of him. "Look at all he gave up."

"I am," Grayson agreed, but his gaze never left the man right in front of him. The scenery was gorgeous, but it didn't compare to the man he had in his arms at that particular moment. God, he wanted to hold him tighter and then turn Tommy around and do his very best to make him forget about Xavier and everything except how amazing he was. The urge was nearly overwhelming, but he held still, his control over his own impulses hanging by a thread.

"Are you cold?" Tommy asked, turning slightly.

"No." Grayson had to get his own body under control as the energy thrummed through him. This, right here, right now, was a dream come true, and it wasn't even real. Yes, Tommy, his best friend, was sitting with him, but all the times Grayson had dreamed of being with Tommy like this, it never included them just being together and nothing else.

"I think I'm going to go in to bed," Tommy said softly and moved away before getting to his feet, rising like a shadow in front of the field of stars.

"Me too." There was no need to stay out here all night. Grayson stood, then followed Tommy down the dock and back through the open sliding doors. He pulled the screen closed and watched as Tommy went to his bedroom.

Tommy paused outside his room, and even though Grayson had no reason to expect it, his spirit did a little skip as Tommy looked back at him. He hoped Tommy would ask him to join him. Even though it wasn't realistic at all, the heart wanted what the heart wanted with no regard for logic at all. "I'm so glad you and Petey are here. I'll see you in the morning."

Grayson nodded and waited until the door to Tommy's room closed. Then he checked all the locks and went to his room. He got ready for bed in the bathroom so he wouldn't wake Petey, then climbed into bed. His body was completely wiped out, but his head had other ideas. He wished he could shut the thing off. Hell, what he wanted was to be able to hold Tommy anytime he wanted, the way he had on the dock. But that was a dream he'd have to forgo. Friends didn't let friends drive drunk, and they certainly didn't jump into bed together, not if they wanted to remain friends for long. That was something Grayson knew very well, and he wasn't angling to repeat that mistake. He kept telling himself it was better to have Tommy as a friend than to mess things up trying for more.

Chapter Three

TOMMY got out of bed, threw on a T-shirt, and walked bleary-eyed into the living room. He didn't want to wake everyone up, but he wasn't going to stay in bed any longer, no matter how much he might have wanted to. It had been years since he'd been able to sleep past six in the morning, and the clock read seven. Of course, with the time change, he was still getting up at six, so what did it matter? He made a pot of coffee, then sat at his computer and logged in to check his messages and answer what he needed to. Then he opened a design window and started laying out some of the basic ideas for the water game he'd thought up. After a cup of coffee, he sank into his work and, as usual, lost track of time.

"Uncle Tommy, are you working?" Petey asked, watching over his shoulder.

"Yes." Tommy didn't look up from the screen, typing as fast as he could.

Petey tsked and patted him on the shoulder. "This is vacation. No working." When Tommy turned, he caught the full-on glare of a nine-year-old filled with righteous indignation.

"I agree with that," Grayson said as he came out of the bedroom in cargo shorts and a tight aquamarine T-shirt.

Tommy turned back to his work because it was easier to pretend to pay attention to the screen than to have Grayson realize Tommy was ogling him. But damn it all, he was most definitely stareworthy. Grayson was tall, broad, and strong. Yesterday in the pool, Tommy had had to concentrate not to drool at his best friend.

"I have to get these ideas down." Tommy saved his work, then made some notes in a file that he saved as well before closing down the computer. "Breakfast?"

"Maybe you better put pants on first," Petey said and then giggled. "You don't want everyone seeing your business." He cracked up at his own joke, and Tommy hurried to his room to change. Tommy rarely paid attention to what he wore in the mornings. His days consisted of getting up and working, stopping only when his stomach or bladder demanded it.

"Sorry, guys," Tommy said when he was showered, dressed, and ready to go.

"I was only teasing," Petey said, hurrying over to give him a hug. Tommy suspected that Grayson had probably had some sort of talk with him while Tommy was away. He hugged Petey in return.

"It's okay. Most of the time I forget when other people are around." He patted Petey's head gently. "Did you sleep well?"

Grayson yawned. "I think Petey did, but I was up and down. You?"

"Same." Tommy yawned and wished he'd had a second cup of coffee. "We'll take it easy today."

"But we can go out in the boat, right?" Petey asked, looking longingly out the window.

Tommy chuckled. Of course, Petey would be a bundle of energy. "I'll arrange for the resort to send a guide this afternoon." That earned a high five, and Tommy was pleased. "Let's go eat."

They left the bungalow, following the path to the main building. It was stucco, the same as the rest of the resort, with high ceilings and fans providing gentle air movement.

Dishes clattered as they got closer to the dining room, which hummed with chatter and excitement. They found a table, and Petey hurried to the buffet.

"You'd swear I never feed him."

Tommy chuckled as he got what he wanted and returned to the table. He requested coffee from the server and sighed when he brought it. He needed the caffeine if he was going to get his body moving. His head was going a million miles an hour and in multiple directions, but his body hadn't caught up yet.

"Is that all you're eating?" Grayson asked, transferring a pancake to Tommy's plate. "Two pieces of bacon and that tiny scoop of eggs?" He shook his head, and Tommy half expected Grayson to take his plate and replace it with his. "You need to eat."

"I'm really not hungry. You filled me up last night so I don't need much." Tommy picked at the food on his plate, taking a few bites of the pancake to make Grayson happy and eating all the bacon, because, well… it was bacon. Grayson added a few pieces to his plate, and Tommy ate those as well before settling back with his coffee. "I'm going back. Take your time, and when you're done, we can go to the market." Tommy excused himself and returned to the bungalow, booted up his computer, and did what he always did when a wave of loneliness washed over him: he threw himself into his work so deeply that nothing else mattered and he could ignore the grief and loss.

TOMMY wasn't sure how long he was alone. Time seemed to stand still. When Grayson and Petey came in, he blinked and checked the time on his computer.

"The resort has an iguana and I got to hold it," Petey said.

"We took a walk around for a while," Grayson explained knowingly. "I also stopped at the front desk and got details and times for the excursions."

Tommy nodded. That was Grayson's way of telling him that Tommy didn't need to worry about any of it. Grayson would make sure they got where they needed to be. Tommy sighed and turned his attention back to the computer screen. "I need a few more minutes and then we can go." He got to work once more, finishing up what he was doing and saving everything, sending his work up to his cloud storage for backup.

"Ready?" Grayson asked as he approached, then rubbed his shoulders. Tommy closed his eyes and soaked in the attention. "You know, you should book a massage so you can let go of all this tension." He dug his fingers in a bit more, working the muscles.

"God, no. You can touch me, but I don't want strangers to." Tommy shuddered. "Maybe that's why—"

"Don't even go there," Grayson practically growled. "We are not going to mention… him… any more this trip. He isn't worth the breath. You had nothing to do with what happened. It was all He Who Shall Not Be Named." Grayson lowered his voice to an ominous depth.

"You're so funny." Tommy couldn't argue with that. He was tired of thinking about Xavier. The guy was a class A ass.

"Can we go now?" Petey asked from the bedroom. He had shorts and a red T-shirt on, with sandals and a hat. "I even put on sunscreen."

Tommy closed the computer, stood, instantly missing the magic from Grayson's fingers, and grabbed his wallet. "Yes. Here's some money." He passed a few bills to Petey. "Now you can buy what you want."

"Tommy," Grayson said, his voice holding a hint of warning.

Tommy spun to face him. "It's my right as an uncle to spoil him." He thrust out his lower lip just enough, knowing Grayson would back down. That look had worked with him for nine years and he knew it. "Come on. There's stuff to see and buy!" Hell, Tommy wasn't averse to a little retail therapy if it did the trick.

The walk to town retraced their steps from the night before, but now the streets bustled with people. A huge white ship was anchored in the port, and groups of people streamed out, heading in all directions. They joined the flow and easily found the market, which consisted of canopies in every color imaginable, with watercolors of sea life, handmade jewelry, local textiles, photographs, and even carvings.

"Dad!" Petey said, racing to a booth with various animals carved from dark wood. "Look at this!" He barely stood still as they approached, then grabbed both of them by the hand to look.

"Each is one of a kind," a middle-aged man with salt-and-pepper hair explained as another man approached him. They didn't touch, but shared a look, and Tommy knew they were together.

"I love this." Petey pointed to a sea turtle and pulled his hand away. The artist lifted the ten-inch carving and handed it to Petey. The detail was extraordinary. The skin of the turtle seemed to ripple as Petey turned it in his hand. It truly was a work of art.

"I don't think you have enough money," Grayson explained as Petey put the turtle back and pulled out all his money from his pocket. "Sorry, buddy."

Tommy turned to Grayson, reaching for his wallet. Grayson never said a word, but his eyes clearly said no. He pulled out his card and waited. Grayson groaned, and Tommy knew he'd won. He handed over a credit card, saying, "He wants the turtle and I want the sea horse." The sea horse was a larger carving, mounted on a piece of coral.

"That was found on the beach at our home. It didn't come from any of the live reefs." He ran the charge, and Tommy signed the iPad screen to complete it. Then the artist packaged the pieces, first in tissue paper and then in bubble wrap. He included a pamphlet for him and bagged both of the pieces.

"How long have you been carving?" Grayson asked.

"All my life." He smiled widely. "I grew up in New York and went to art school. Cass and I came down here ten years ago on vacation, fell in love with the place, and never left. We dive and snorkel at least once a week, and I carve what I see. I'm working on a larger piece for the new community hall."

"It's an entire school of fish, and each one is different," Cass explained, clearly proud. "There are hundreds of them."

Other people approached the booth, and they stepped back, waving and saying goodbye before moving on.

Grayson carried the bags with their purchases, and Tommy once again fell into a funk. He had imagined that he and Xavier would be happy the way those two were. Tommy had had visions of them growing older together, traveling, spending time together. But it wasn't to be, and he needed to stop moping about it. It wasn't helping anyone. Xavier was gone, and Tommy was better off.

"T-shirts." Petey hurried down the walk to the bright shop. "I want to get one with a turtle on it." He disappeared into the shop, and Tommy smiled, letting go of the slump that had settled on him. How could he possibly be gloomy with Petey along to add youthful energy and happiness?

"All right," Grayson said, then added to Tommy, "You know that wasn't necessary."

Tommy stopped. "So I was going to buy the piece I wanted and not get his?" he asked, putting his hands on his hips. "It made me happy."

Grayson pursed his lips and then shook his head, the hint of a smile forming. "How am I going to teach him that he can't have everything he sees when you buy him whatever he wants?"

"It's just this week while we're on vacation. I have more money than I can possibly spend in a lifetime, and getting him—and you, if I want—something to remember this trip by is special to me." He blinked and swore under his breath. He was not going to do this here in the middle of the fucking street. Tommy closed his eyes to ward off the wave of extreme loneliness that threatened to enshroud him.

"Okay," Grayson agreed, motioning toward the shop. They found Petey looking at a light blue T-shirt with a turtle on the back. "That's nice. Just make sure it's your size." Petey showed him the label, and Grayson spread it out on his back to make sure it would fit. "Okay."

"Can I get two?"

"Yes. But you have to show them to me before you pay," Grayson said. He walked through the shop to find the bathing suits, picked one out, and held it up.

"I don't think that's your size," Tommy teased. "Your junk won't fit."

Grayson looked him over. "This is for you. That one you have doesn't fit, and this will look nice." He handed it to Tommy and continued shopping. Apparently they were on some sort of "clothe Tommy" spree. Grayson grabbed a few T-shirts, as well as a pair of shorts, and had Tommy try them on. Then he took them and headed for the register. Before Tommy could stop him, Grayson had paid for everything and helped Petey with his purchases. Then Grayson handed him the bag and leaned close. "You're an attractive man. You should have some things to show it off a little."

Tommy scoffed under his breath. He knew the truth about how he looked.

They left the store and wandered the rest of the way through the town, but there wasn't a great deal else to see. The scenery and attractions on Bonaire were clearly mostly on and in the water.

"Can I get some candy?" Petey asked as they passed a store with a display in the window.

"No," Tommy said gently as Grayson shook his head. "We'll have lunch in an hour." He turned to Grayson. "I got so caught up in work, I forgot to arrange for someone to take us out in the boat."

"I did it. They'll be ready for us at three." Grayson smiled. "I got your back." He patted Tommy on the shoulder. "How about something cold to drink?"

"Yes!" Petey said enthusiastically, and they found a café and got something to drink, sitting in the shade of a thatched roof with open sides to catch the near constant breeze. It truly was a paradise on earth, and by the time they got back to the bungalow, Tommy was happy and felt no desire to open his computer.

THEY had a nice lunch by the pool once again. Petey played in the water for hours and only got out because it was getting close to the time for boating.

"It's warm, so you'll want your bathing suit," Grayson said, and Tommy went to his room, pulled out the new suit, and changed into it and one of the new T-shirts. When he stepped out, Grayson stared at him, smiling and nodding. "You look good." For a second Tommy thought he might have seen heat in Grayson's eyes, but he dismissed it, even as his dick stirred in his suit.

"So do you," he told Grayson as he pulled open the patio door, and they stepped out on the dock.

They waited for only a minute when a man approached, carrying a cooler, swinging it a little as he walked. "Johan, we weren't expecting you," Tommy said, shaking the hand of their bartender and server from lunch the previous day.

"I tend to do a little of everything, and since I know all the best spots, they asked me to take you." Johan climbed onto the boat and set the cooler down. "I have drinks and snacks if you want it." He put up the sun shade and checked over the boat before starting the engine, casting off the lines, and zipping away from the dock. "As you know, this is Bonaire, and over there is Klein Bonaire. Most of the reefs and water around the island are protected. In some places I can take you closer to shore, but we have to stay away from certain locations." Johan pointed to a floating orange shape. "See that buoy? It means that a diver is under the water there." He gave it a wide berth.

"How fast does the boat go?" Petey asked.

"Let's find out," Johan answered, opening her up. They zoomed over the water, wind and spray zipping past. Tommy sat back, hoping he didn't get seasick, but after a few minutes, all he felt was excitement. "All of Klein Bonaire is protected, so you won't find WaveRunners or jet skis there. They're banned. Even people who had them before the law can't have them any longer. It's to protect the sea life." He slowed down some. "There are no rivers or lakes on Bonaire, so there is no runoff into the sea. So without the silt in the water, the corals and sponges grow faster and the water is clearer than just about any other place on earth."

"Can you camp on the small island?"

"Sometimes, but there is nothing there at all and it's heavily regulated. Stuff washes up all the time, and in a few months, a group of us are organizing an island cleanup. We'll go to Klein Bonaire and remove as much trash and debris as we safely can. Everything we do helps keep the reefs healthy." Johan pointed to something red in the plants near the shore. "A cooler someone lost overboard and didn't bother to try to retrieve." He cut the engines further as they got closer to the island. "Look over the side," he said as he slowed to a near stop.

Tommy leaned over carefully and gasped. As the water cleared on the lee side of the boat, a world opened up under them. Brightly colored fish in yellow and blue darted under them, above a seabed filled with brownish yellow and orange. Fans swayed back and forth with the current.

"A turtle," Petey called, pointing. Sure enough, a small sea turtle broke the surface near the boat and went back down. "Can we see more?"

"Sure. The best way is to snorkel, and I understand you're doing that with Woodwind in a few days. They're the best, so the resort uses them for their excursions instead of organizing them themselves. You'll see everything." Johan spoke directly to Petey. "The last time I was out, I saw a small octopus and a sea horse. But you have to be pretty eagle-eyed because they like to hide."

"Cool," Petey said, clearly enthralled.

Johan backed the boat up and turned it around, heading away from the island.

Tommy took a seat in the shade, and Grayson sat next to him while Petey stood near Johan, talking away. "This is stunning," Tommy observed. He closed his eyes and leaned slightly. Grayson was there, sliding an arm around him, and Tommy soaked up the attention. He had no illusions that it was anything more than caring friendship, but he liked it. Grayson smelled of spice and salt water. It was hot, and he did his best not to overreact.

The truth was, he'd had a crush on Grayson for years. But Grayson had never made a move. More than once Tommy had kicked himself for not being more forward. And the one time he had actually screwed up the courage to ask someone out, it had turned out to be Xavier, and, well, that had turned into a pile of crap.

He turned slightly and saw Grayson looking back at him. Tommy swallowed hard as he gazed into Grayson's blue eyes. They were so familiar and yet different. He'd never seen them this dark, the color of the deepest water around them. He'd call them stunning if he saw them casually, but right now they were like large pools that beckoned to him, and he wanted to get lost in their depths forever.

"Dad, look," Petey called, and Grayson turned, his arm sliding away. "Dolphins." Petey pointed to the front of the boat, where a pair were riding along with them. "That's so cool."

Tommy pulled out his phone and snapped pictures, catching one as it leaped out of the water. He photographed the surrounding area and took pictures of Grayson and Petey as they stood together, watching the clowns of the sea. When they turned around, he snapped a final picture and sat back down, listening, hoping to catch some of Petey's excitement.

"Just relax. You don't need to try to force yourself to be happy," Grayson told him, sidling up next to him with understanding in his eyes.

Tommy relaxed and lay back on the bench in the shade. The engine hummed and the boat rocked. Petey's, Grayson's, and Johan's voices swirled around him, but he ignored them. He hadn't slept well, and soon his fatigue took over. The voices and hum grew distant. He still heard them, but paid no attention. He just relaxed and let go of his hold on consciousness.

"Is he asleep?" Petey asked. Tommy probably would have smiled, but he was too relaxed and kept his eyes closed.

"I hope so. He never sleeps much."

"Do you think I can drive the boat?" Petey asked, and he heard footsteps and then Johan giving instructions. "Look, Dad, I'm doing it!"

Tommy knew Johan was nearby and zoned out further, glad Petey was having fun.

"ARE you awake now?" Petey asked as Tommy stretched.

"Yes." He sat up, blinking behind his sunglasses. "Where are we?"

"On the far side of Klein Bonaire." Grayson sat next to him. "Petey asked if we could take a trip around the island. We'll head back in from there."

Tommy turned to where Petey stood behind the wheel of the boat, with Johan next to him. "You're doing a good job."

"I like this. Dad, can we get a boat?" Petey asked.

"He's asked for everything he's seen," Grayson said. "I blame you."

Tommy grinned. "Sure, Petey. Your dad will buy you a boat. Though it will be much smaller. Probably bathtub-sized."

"Uncle Tommy...." Petey turned back to steering, and Tommy settled in for the ride.

Grayson nudged his shoulder after a while. "Are you sure you're okay?"

Tommy nodded. "Yeah. I guess I needed some rest." He sat back, content just to be for a while. "I keep going back to that asshole. I know I shouldn't, but he's there in my mind." He rummaged in his pocket for his phone. Of course, there was no signal. But he added a reminder to call his parents just to check in. His mom and dad would be worried. "I know that I'll be fine eventually and that his leaving isn't the end of the world."

"Just enjoy yourself," Grayson told him. "Relax and have some fun."

They rounded the edge of the island, the larger one coming back into view. It was breathtaking and so natural. Only the main town with the port area marred the view. Otherwise it looked like an unspoiled paradise.

Tommy slid closer, leaning on Grayson. He'd done that a lot, but Grayson didn't seem to mind, and he needed some support at the moment. He settled in when Grayson put his arm around him, and they rode all the way back to the dock that way.

"You should date," Tommy said as they got close.

"What brought that on?" Grayson asked.

"I don't know. I've just been thinking that you're a great guy and that you should have someone wonderful in your life." Just because his dream had gone up in flames didn't mean Grayson shouldn't have someone. "You deserve someone to love you and help take care of Petey. Someone who will think the sun rises and sets on both of you."

They drew closer to the dock, and Johan took control, slowing the boat once again.

"I have someone already for all of that," Grayson said softly, squeezing Tommy slightly. For a second he was jealous, wondering who Grayson was seeing and why he wouldn't tell him. Then Tommy thought that maybe Grayson was talking about him. But before he could ask, they were docking and Grayson stood to try to help. Then they gathered their things, exited the boat, and walked the short distance to their bungalow.

"Thanks, Johan, that was totally awesome." They all shared a high five.

"Just call down when you want to go out again. Maybe next time we could go the other direction." Johan waved and carried the now nearly empty cooler with him.

"What are we going to do now?" Petey asked.

"I think Uncle Tommy is going to rest, and I want to do the same. So you can play video games or watch television for a while. We've spent a lot of time outside and in the sun, so some quiet time to cool off is a good idea." Grayson pulled open the bungalow door, and they stepped inside.

The cool interior surrounded him, and Tommy flopped down on the sofa, instantly wrung out. He hoped Petey played by himself for a while. "I'm going to get something to drink and then lie down." He didn't have any more energy to be around people... anyone, at the moment. "Call me when it's time for dinner."

"Sure," Grayson said.

Tommy pulled himself to his feet and grabbed a bottle of water, then went to his room and closed the door. He loved that he had a king-sized bed. He only wished he wasn't sleeping in it alone. The room was big, bright, airy, and just what he'd expect in the tropics. The colors were cool and gentle. He took off his sunglasses and kicked off his sandals, then lay down on top of the bedding, letting the ceiling fan stir the air. In the best of times, he needed quiet moments, but with everything that had happened in the last few days, he really needed to hibernate for a while.

The pillows and bedding were top-notch, soft, and cool. He closed his eyes and willed his mind not to think about Xavier, but instead to concentrate on schools of fish, dolphins, sea turtles, and everything else he'd seen. That was what he wanted to dwell on. Let the tropics soothe away the aches and pain for a while. He closed his eyes and did just that, allowing the calm he needed to sweep over him. Maybe he'd feel better once he'd truly had a chance to rest. Tommy sighed as if it were ever that easy.

He didn't sleep long, but he relaxed, and once he got up, he found Grayson and Petey at the pool. Petey tried to coax him in, but he sat in the lounge and watched, the game idea churning through his head. He so wanted to work on it, but he knew he had enough of the initial design idea down in his notes that he wasn't going to lose track of it. He could just relax now.

A server stopped by, and he ordered a Polar and enjoyed his beer as he watched the others play. Okay, mostly he watched Grayson, because he was too droolworthy not to look at. Grayson played with Petey for a while and then headed for the stairs. The water ran down his chest as he rose out of the pool. God, he was gorgeous, with everything Tommy didn't have. Grayson worked out, so his chest was broad and full. He had lean, narrow hips and a sprinkling of dark hair on golden skin. He smiled as he turned to Tommy and headed over, grabbing one of the towels and using it to dry himself before sitting next to him.

"Did you rest?"

"Some. I feel a lot better now." Tommy lay back, glancing over at Grayson when he didn't think he was looking. He needed to let go of this fascination he seemed to be developing for Grayson right alongside pushing Xavier out of his life. "I thought we'd get dinner here tonight. I don't really feel up to going anywhere, and tomorrow we have our first snorkel trip, so rest is going to be important."

Petey got out of the pool and hurried over. "That kid took my gun." He turned and pointed to a kid who must have been about fourteen and was a lot bigger than Petey.

Grayson stood, walked over to him as though he owned the pool, and got back the water gun, intimidating the hell out of the kid. Grayson handed Petey back the toy, but it seemed the real fun in the pool was over, and Petey came back to sit next to Tommy.

"Why would he do that? I said he could use it for a while, but I didn't give it to him." Petey pulled a towel over himself, and Tommy knew just how he felt. He'd been bullied plenty in his life.

"Some people think that because they're bigger, they get to do whatever they want. It's all right, though. Your dad took care of it, and that kid will leave you alone from now on." Tommy liked that Grayson stood up for Petey. He also liked the way Grayson had thrown his chest out, drawing himself up to his full height as he approached the kid.

"Good." He put his guns beside the chair and curled up under the towel.

"Do you want to go inside? Are you getting hungry?" Tommy asked.

"Do we have any juice?"

Tommy flagged down a server and ordered Petey some orange juice. When he brought the glass, Petey downed it quickly. One thing Tommy was discovering was that in this heat, drinking a lot was a requirement.

"I talked to his dad," Grayson said when he rejoined them. "He and his wife are going through a divorce and she gives him everything he wants, so he's coming to expect it from everyone. Apparently he'd asked for one of those guns and his dad had told him no."

"Well, he can't have mine. That's not fair."

Grayson ruffled Petey's hair. "That's right. But it was nice of you to let him use one." He sat down, and they grew quiet as the shadows lengthened. "Let's get inside so we can all get changed out of our wet clothes. Uncle Tommy is going to order dinner, and we can have it delivered to our bungalow."

"Like room service?" Petey seemed fascinated with that.

"Exactly." Tommy stood, waiting for the others. He let them go first because it was polite, but then he realized an excellent side benefit: he got to ogle Grayson's tight bubble butt in his wet clingy suit without him seeing him. Okay, so he'd figure out how to let this thing about Grayson go tomorrow.

While they changed, Tommy looked over the menu and then found out what everyone wanted before calling in the order. There were games in the cabinet in the living room, so they set up and played Trouble until the food arrived. Tommy's appetite seemed to have returned full force, and he ate his steak and potatoes with unabashed relish, then sat back in his chair, stuffed to the gills and happy. After clearing the table, they played another game, which Petey won easily, and then he got ready for bed.

Just like the previous evening, Tommy found Grayson out on the dock, looking at the stars. He joined him, and Grayson wound his arms around Tommy's waist.

"I love the start of trips. All the fun is ahead and there's still everything to look forward to."

Grayson held him a little tighter, and Tommy wanted to ask him about it, but he was a little afraid to also. God, he hated that. All his life he'd wondered about this handsome guy or that one who made him laugh, but he'd never done anything about it until Xavier. He'd always felt somewhat like a coward.

"Grayson," Tommy whispered and slowly turned around. He couldn't make out his eyes, other than to tell they were half-lidded. He did see the way Grayson's lips were parted and caught a peek of his tongue as it slid across them.

"Yes," Grayson whispered, and Tommy wasn't sure if he was being given the green light, but it was now or never, so he closed the distance between them to kiss his best friend.

Holy hell, if this was how it felt to kiss a friend, Tommy should have done it years ago. Grayson leaned forward, deepening the kiss, winding his fingers through Tommy's hair. The lap of the water and the calls of the birds all fell away as the pounding of his heart in his ears grew to a crescendo. Grayson guided him, turning him fully, pulling Tommy close, devouring his lips, sending enough heat racing through Tommy to scorch the dock below them.

Tommy pulled back. He had to see Grayson, who cupped his cheeks, holding him still, not letting Tommy get away. He inhaled deeply, struggling for air. "Oh God," Tommy gasped under his breath.

"Is that good or bad?" Grayson asked.

"Do you really have to ask?" Tommy closed the distance between them once again, pushing Grayson back against the piling with a thud. Grayson groaned, and Tommy chuckled, rubbing the back of Grayson's head, fingers carding through his soft hair to make him feel better before kissing him once again.

"I guess not." Grayson's chuckle came through clearly as he held Tommy close.

"Dad," Petey called from inside. Tommy backed away, and Grayson stood to head toward the bungalow. Tommy got up as well, then followed him up to the patio door.

"What is it?" Grayson asked.

"Are there scorpions here?" Petey asked. "One of the kids at the pool said he saw a scorpion today. Do I have to shake out my shoes in the morning?"

Grayson pulled open the door, and Petey stepped outside in pajama shorts, carrying Grayson's phone. "No. There aren't any on the island. In fact, have you noticed that there aren't any insects? There isn't a place for most of them to breed. The screens are to keep out the lizards, which will get everywhere if you let them." He took his phone away. "Now go on back to bed." He was so patient, and that made Tommy wonder if that was just the kind of lover Grayson would be too.

"Are you coming too?" Petey asked.

Grayson turned to him, and Tommy saw him sigh. "I'll be in the room in a few minutes, so go on to bed." He turned to Tommy as Petey went inside. "I need to see to him. For some reason, some of those kids at the pool tried to scare him."

"It's all right. I'll see you in the morning." Tommy figured he wasn't going to sleep again tonight, but for a very different reason than last night.

Grayson leaned forward to kiss him again before joining Petey in the bedroom. Part of Tommy resented Petey's interruption, but how in the heck could he be jealous of Grayson's son? Petey was a great kid, and Tommy knew Grayson was a father first and foremost. It was part of the deal, which was as it should be. Maybe that was why he hadn't had any long-term relationships.

Tommy waited until the other bedroom door closed before making sure everything was closed up for the night, then tried to go to bed himself. It took a while for the taste of Grayson to fade, but Tommy finally got to sleep with no hint of Xavier in his dreams.

Chapter Four

GRAYSON heard Tommy in the other room and quietly got out of bed. Hopefully Petey would sleep a while longer. Grayson made sure the curtains were pulled to keep the room as dark as possible before dressing hastily. He had thought to sneak out of the room and go to Tommy once Petey was asleep, but he stopped himself. First, Petey would get worried if he woke and Grayson wasn't there when Petey expected him to be. And he and Tommy had shared a kiss. It was an earth-shattering kiss that sent tingles up Grayson's spine just thinking about it. But the kiss hadn't come with an invitation to join Tommy in his bed, and Grayson hadn't wanted to be so forward.

Grayson knew he needed to be careful. He wasn't going to make the same mistake with Tommy that he'd made with Jeffrey. That had cost him so much, including a close friend who would no longer speak to him.

He opened the door and went into the living room, drawn to the scent of coffee that filled the room. "I swear you live on caffeine," Grayson said after silently closing the door.

"Nectar of the gods," Tommy quipped, lifting his mug and then setting it down once again, returning his attention to the computer. "I'm almost done here."

"How long have you been up?" Grayson poured some coffee and carried the mug out to the patio door and onto the dock.

"Couple hours." Tommy typed quickly and then the keys silenced, followed by the snick of the laptop closing. Tommy walked up behind him and then sat down, their feet dangling off the dock above the water. "Umm, last night... I...."

Grayson didn't look away from the water for fear of what he'd see in Tommy's eyes. "If you decide to placate me with some platitudes, I'm going to shove you into the water." He sipped from the mug and waited for some response.

Tommy got up from next to him, and Grayson figured he'd go inside and neither of them would ever talk about the kiss for the rest of their lives. If that was how Tommy wanted it, then it was something Grayson would live with.

"Oh," he groaned as Tommy's hands rested on his shoulders, then worked down the muscles to his arms. "That's good."

"I know. I learned from the best." Tommy got the muscles loosened and slipped his hands under the collar of Grayson's open shirt. Tommy slid his palms over Grayson's chest, not stopping until Grayson quivered.

He leaned back to give Tommy more access and closed his eyes, wanting to concentrate on the sensation.

"Who was that master of touch?" Grayson teased.

Tommy gently withdrew his hands, sliding his fingers around the back of Grayson's neck. "Smartass," Tommy said softly. "And let's get something straight before we go any further."

"What's that?" Grayson asked.

Tommy lightly took his ear with his fingers. "Sometimes you can be a real ass. That's something you can work on." He let go and then lightly kissed Grayson's ear.

"I can do that, as long as you…." Grayson's words faded into giggles as Tommy wriggled his fingers along his side.

"Dad," Petey called groggily, and Tommy turned toward the voice. "You're making noise, and there are kids trying to sleep here."

"Sorry. Go back to bed," Grayson said, then covered his mouth. Tommy did the same because, damn, that was way too funny. "See what you did?" Grayson whispered.

"I can still hear you," Petey said in a singsong way.

"Then it's time for you to get up." Grayson stood, and Tommy did the same. He very much wanted to continue where things were headed, but….

"It's all right. I understand you don't want Petey to know," Tommy told him.

Grayson nodded. There wasn't anything to know yet. But if he knew his son, Petey would be happy as anything, and if things didn't work out, then Petey would get hurt. And Grayson didn't want that—he couldn't have that. Petey and Jeffrey had been friends. A few times before they'd been dating, Jeffrey had taken Petey for a few days because Grayson had had to travel for work. Petey always came home singing Jeffrey's praises, telling Grayson all the things they'd done together. So when things ended badly with Jeffrey, Petey had been the one to get hurt the most. "Thank you." He squeezed Tommy's hand and then went inside.

"I'm hungry, Dad." Petey rubbed his eyes.

"Then you need to get dressed. You can't go to breakfast in BB-8 pajamas." Petey was nuts for anything Star Wars, at least this month. He had tried to convince Tommy to create a Star Wars game, but Tommy couldn't without paying a fortune for the rights.

Petey ambled over to give Grayson a hug. "Are you and Uncle Tommy going to be doing the horizontal hula? 'Cause, you know, it's okay. I like Uncle Tommy, and then he'd really be my uncle."

"Where did you learn things like that?" Grayson had to ask, shaking his head.

"Dad...." Petey drew the word out like Grayson was stupid. "I know all about sex and stuff. Gees, I'm not a baby." He turned to walk away, then stopped. "Oh, and is it okay if I think I like girls and not boys like you and Uncle Tommy?"

Grayson nodded, swallowing hard. Dammit, where was his little boy going? This was way too soon for all of this. "Of course. You can like whoever you like." Good Lord. He hoped to hell Tommy wasn't outside listening to this. He'd probably wet himself from trying not to laugh.

"Okay. Can we eat now?"

Grayson waved him off to change, and Petey hurried into the bedroom. Grayson drank the last of his coffee. He was going to need a heck of a lot more if he was going to be having these conversations in the near future.

"Tommy, we're getting ready for breakfast," Grayson said and waited for him to come in. When he did, Tommy was as red as if he'd been sunburned.

"Horizontal hula," he snickered.

"I know. I don't think I'm ready for this. He's going to get older, go on dates, and God, then I have to have the safe-sex talk and make sure he does everything right." How was he going to get through all that?

"Breathe. He's nine, and you have plenty of time before any of that happens. But maybe you could talk things over with his mother when you see her next. Let her tell him all about girls. She is one, after all."

"You're having way too much fun with this." Grayson swatted Tommy on the butt. "Go get showered and dressed so we can all get something to eat. We're going to need our energy for snorkeling this afternoon."

"I've been thinking about that." Tommy took a step back. "You and Petey go, and I'll stay here and work."

"No," Grayson said softly. "How about you come with us and I'll hold your hand so nothing happens to you?" He moved closer. "I know you aren't comfortable in the water all the time, but this is something really special. All those things we saw from the boat, you'll be able to view firsthand, and more. So please come with us." It was his turn to do that thing with his lower lip, and damned if he didn't see Tommy cave almost instantly.

"I'll come, but not because of the pouty lip." Tommy into his bedroom and closed the door.

Grayson snorted and went to get ready for the day himself.

BREAKFAST was great, and afterward they spent part of the morning watching a movie and being quiet.

It was good for Petey to have some chill time. Tommy worked, and Grayson half watched the movie and spent the other half the time watching Tommy. Now that his attraction was out in the open, he wasn't shy about looking.

"Dad. This is the best part." They were watching *The Force Awakens* for the eighth time, and the planet was about to explode.

Grayson turned back to the movie for a few minutes and then looked away again.

Petey poked him. "Dad. Quit making goo-goo eyes at Uncle Tommy and watch the movie."

Grayson grabbed Petey and pushed him back on the sofa, going for the ticklish spots. Rather than arguing with him, he'd tickle Petey into submission. Peals of laughter rang through the bungalow.

"I'm gonna woof," Petey protested between bouts of laughter, and Grayson backed off before resuming the tickling once again.

"Can I make goo-goo eyes at Uncle Tommy now?" Grayson asked, sitting back up. Petey was still laughing as he reached for the remote to back the movie up a scene and watch the best part all over again.

"The ending of the movie is kinda lame," Petey said once the credits rolled.

"How so?" Grayson was interested in what Petey saw, and Tommy paused in his work, pushing his chair away from the desk before joining them.

"Yeah, let's have it."

Petey bounced on the sofa, clearly getting excited. "So, they spend all this time trying to get BB-8 away from the First Order because he has part of the map to Luke, right? And when the Alliance gets it, they don't recognize what they have. So instead of looking for the rest of the map, they go off and destroy the Starkiller Base… and then—" He waved his hands over his head. "—ta-da, R2-D2 wakes up and he has the rest of the map. Wham, bam, they put them together and everything is hunky-dory." Petey opened his mouth, sticking his finger in it. "Come on. Someone just needed to bang R2-D2 in the head and tell him to cough it up." He was clearly wound up. "And then… ta-da again… the maps fit perfectly…." He looked at both of them. "See? Lame." He sat back on the sofa, crossing his arms across his chest like he expected an argument. "I don't wanna see that movie again… at least not until the next one comes out."

Tommy chuckled and stayed where he was. "I'm tired of working." He put his hands behind his head, relaxing, as Grayson nearly slipped off the sofa. Those were words he never expected to hear from Tommy.

"Is it time to eat?" Petey asked, rubbing his belly. "I want chicken nuggets, I think."

"We'll go in an hour or so, and from there we can catch our boat. It leaves from the other side of the resort, so we don't have far to go." Grayson got up, straightening. "Come on. You need to put your things away," he added to Petey, whose idea of cleaning was to throw everything in his closet at home. "Put your dirty clothes in the suitcase beside my bed."

Petey raced around, taking care of his things and putting all his pool things in the new bag Grayson had brought for wet stuff. "Can we go swimming?" he asked, clearly restless.

"Okay. Put on your suit, and I'll go out and watch you." Grayson walked to where Tommy sat. "Are you going to come with us or do you need some quiet time?"

"I'll come."

Grayson leaned down to kiss Tommy quickly, then went to change into his bathing suit.

Petey had a ball in the pool, even managing to coax them both into the water for a while. They had a nice lunch while their suits dried, then gathered their things and went to catch the boat.

"It has sails," Petey said, bouncing on his heels.

"All right. Relax," Grayson said, handing Petey his bag to give him something to do as Tommy checked them in.

"Welcome to Woodwind," a tall, lean, light mahogany woman said. She was quite stunning and looked like she had spent her entire life in the water. "I'm Alena, and this is our afternoon sail. We're going to have a lot of fun. We should have everything you need for an amazing time. Once we get on board and underway, we'll fit each of you with masks, fins, snorkels. We have wetsuits and sun shirts if you want them, as well as corrective lens masks." She motioned, and the entire group of nearly twenty people made their way down the dock to the catamaran.

She and her crew helped everyone on board and got them situated before setting sail, and once underway, they proceeded to set everyone up with all the equipment they were going to need. Grayson got Tommy, Petey, and himself wetsuits. They were going to be spending three hours in the water, so he figured that was safest. Once he had Petey all set, he made sure Tommy had everything he needed. "He's a nervous swimmer," Grayson told Alena quietly.

"No problem. We'll put the three of you with me in the third group, and I can help you." She smiled as though that was something she did every day... and it probably was.

They served drinks of various juices, water, and sodas. Grayson made sure Petey stuck to juice and helped get him and Tommy slathered with sunscreen. He got helped in return, and as Tommy rubbed the lotion around his face, his wetsuit grew a little tighter. Grayson hoped this turned out to be as much fun as he envisioned. "You need to drink a lot to keep hydrated," he told Petey, who leaned in and stage-whispered.

"But what if I have to pee?"

"The bathroom is right down those stairs," Alena said. "Just be careful and go down backward." Obviously she had answered that question many times before. She stood near the mast and introduced all of the crew and Ricardo, the photographer, who would take pictures of their trip that they could buy at the end.

They sailed to the first stop just off Klein Bonaire, and each group got into the water. Grayson got his mask on and helped Petey with his. When it was their turn, they carefully got into the water, then floated as the current moved them forward. Grayson stayed with Petey and Tommy, holding Tommy's hand. At first Tommy seemed nervous, but after a few minutes, relaxation settled in.

They floated over a seabed that looked like something out of a nature special. Coral in red, yellow, gold, and brown formed a backdrop for fish of blue, yellow, and silver that darted everywhere. Petey swam up next to him, and Grayson took his hand as well, the three of them together exploring a new world.

Petey pointed, and Grayson could feel his excitement as a sea turtle glided near deeper water. Tommy nodded as well, then pointed as a small octopus skittered along the bottom away from them. Grayson tightened his grip on Petey's hand, afraid he was going to want to swim after it.

They surfaced and Grayson checked with Tommy. "Are you okay?"

Tommy spat out his snorkel. "This is amazing."

Petey had the same reaction. They positioned their snorkels and went under again.

What surprised Grayson was how quiet it was. He heard the sound of his own breathing and that was about it. Everything else was the humming of a soft breeze. He was basically alone with his thoughts and his view of the undersea world, unlike anything he'd ever seen before.

Alena dove to show them anemones and urchins, even a sea horse, which Grayson knew would make Tommy happy. Petey pointed as a shark glided off to the side, way too small to be a threat. The photographer dove ahead of them, taking their pictures, and when Petey pointed, he snapped pictures of the shark, as well as the little black sea horse. Tommy squeezed his hand, and he returned it while Petey let go and floated nearby on his own. For a few minutes, it was just the two of them in an undersea world that took Grayson's breath away.

All too soon it was time to get out. They got their fins off and climbed the ladder. Petey pulled off his mask, then proceeded to tell them about everything they'd seen and hugged Uncle Tommy for bringing them here. More juice was served as they sailed to a new location and then got back into the water for a second and eventually a third time.

"Do you want some help?" Alena asked Tommy, who smiled.

"I'm actually doing really good." He looked thoughtful for a moment, then said, "We're booked on another excursion on Wednesday through the resort. Do you know if it visits the same spots?"

"No. That one is all afternoon, and they go to some other spots on Bonaire, so you'll see different things."

"Cool," Petey said as they got ready for their fourth drift snorkel.

This reef was different. Tall sponges reached for the surface, swaying in the current. Fans and tubes moved with the water. Once again, Grayson held Tommy's hand, and Alena took Petey with her, so the two of them had time alone. Another sea turtle made an appearance. This one was large, gliding close and then rolling onto his side as he banked away. It was stunningly beautiful. If Grayson could have kissed Tommy, he would have. But instead he squeezed his fingers as they slowly moved over the reef.

When they got out, their equipment was collected, and Grayson pulled towels out of his bag for Petey and Tommy, as well as himself, followed by shirts to protect them from the sun. Once they were reasonably dry and reslathered with sunscreen, they drank more juice, this time spiked with a little rum for him and Tommy. Plates of amazing noodles with vegetables and chicken were distributed to everyone.

"I don't want this to end," Tommy said, leaning against him. When he looked in Grayson's direction again, Tommy's gaze grew volcano hot, and sweat broke out on Grayson's back just from his expression. Words seemed inadequate, so neither spoke, and Grayson shifted closer.

The photographer came around, and Grayson dug out some money from his bag and bought a turtle-shaped drive with all the pictures on it from the excursion. He definitely wanted the ones of the three of them.

By the time they reached the dock, the sun was getting low in the sky. Tommy and Petey were talking nonstop about everything, feeding off each other's excitement. They disembarked, and Tommy put a nice tip in the bucket.

"See you Wednesday," Petey told Alena, then hugged her. "This was awesome, and you even got

Uncle Tommy in the water. He's like a big chicken."
He turned and raced back to them.

"Did you really have to say that?" Tommy asked.

"But you are, like, Chicken of the Sea or
something." Petey giggled. "But that's okay, though.
You aren't scared anymore. Are you?"

"Nope. You got me over it." Tommy ruffled Petey's
hair as they headed back to their bungalow.

Grayson was exhilarated and exhausted. His belly
was full and he wanted to rest. He also wanted it to
be bedtime so he could spend some alone time with
Tommy and maybe a little bed time with him as well.
Passion thrummed through him, and every time he
turned to Tommy, he saw him looking back, banked
heat simmering in his gaze.

"Are we gonna have dinner?" Petey asked.

"You just ate."

Petey rolled his eyes. "That was a snack."

"How about we get changed and then we can eat?
After that, you'll have to go to bed. There's more fun on
tap for tomorrow and you don't want to miss it."

"Can we go out in the boat again?" Petey asked.

"You can do whatever you want." God, it felt good
to be able to say that. This trip was exactly what all
three of them needed, and it was turning out damn near
perfect. Tommy hadn't mentioned or even alluded to
Xavier all day. His gazes told Grayson that he had ideas
that might involve some naked bed time, and more than
anything, he and Tommy had made some memories
that neither of them were ever likely to forget.

THEY had dinner near the pool under lights with
calypso music playing. Couples danced, and Grayson

was even able to coax Tommy out onto the floor, if only for a few minutes. Petey laughed and joined them, and they had a family dance that tickled some of the other guests. By the time they got back to the bungalow, Petey was half-asleep, and it took only a few minutes before he was in bed and out like a light. Grayson brushed his teeth and left the bedroom, closing the door, wondering what the night had in store yet, if anything.

He and Tommy hadn't exactly talked about anything regarding what was going to happen. He realized he'd gotten his engines running—okay, revving—based solely on some looks and touches. He sat on the sofa and wondered if all of this was in his head. Maybe it was what he wanted to see, so he'd made sure it was there. Grayson didn't even know if Tommy was going to come out of his room or not. He thought about turning on the television to give him something to do, but then Tommy pulled his door open and stepped into the room.

"What is it?" Grayson asked at the pained look.

"Shit, I don't know." Tommy ran a hand through his hair, then closed the door and sat down. "We've been friends a long time, and I don't want to do anything to mess that up." He swallowed. "I remember how things were with Jeffrey. You were close. Not as close as we are, but close. You went on vacations together and things like that. Then you got serious and everything went to hell."

Grayson couldn't argue with that. "Did I ever tell you why I broke things off?"

"Not really. I know it was hard for you. But I was traveling then and wasn't around. After that, you didn't want to talk about it, so I left it alone."

Grayson scoffed softly. "Yeah. That sounds like me." He turned toward the bedroom. "Like you said, Jeffrey and I had known each other for years, and I thought we understood each other. But we didn't, not really. Once we started dating, he couldn't understand why I wouldn't go out on Saturdays and stay out all night. He wanted me to get babysitters or send Petey to my parents so we could have a good time. To him, Petey was someone in his way, and he could never understand that Petey had to come first. So when he gave me an ultimatum, I made the only choice I'd ever make, and that was the end of that. I said I thought we could be friends, but he wasn't interested and moved on." Grayson sighed softly. "I thought that he was a good friend and that he'd be someone who would love Petey, but that wasn't to be."

"You know I adore Petey," Tommy said.

"I do. But being around him a few times a week is different from living with him and being an everyday part of his life. He's a kid, with all the ups and downs they have." Not that Grayson would trade being a father for anything. "When I first found out about Petey, I was terrified, and then Anne wanted to leave him with me. Petey wasn't quite three. Anne is many things, but she isn't particularly maternal, which is fine. She has other amazing qualities, and it was my responsibility to be a father." He leaned forward. "Like I said, I was terrified, but as soon as I got to know him, that was it." He lifted his gaze. "If Anne came back and said that she wanted custody of him again, I'd fight her tooth and nail and probably rip her to pieces if I had to. Petey is my son and the most important person in my life, and always will be."

"I know that. You know my mom. She was like a tiger when it came to me. No one pulled anything because they'd have her to deal with. I was the center of her world because I was the only child she was ever going to have, and I suspect Petey will be your only child." Tommy shifted, gently rubbing Grayson's back. "You don't have to worry that I'm going to suddenly turn all needy and self-centered."

"I didn't think that about Jeffrey either." Grayson closed his eyes, soaking in Tommy's attention. It was hard to admit that sometimes he wished there was someone to pay some attention to him. Grayson was always looking after Petey, and that was how it should be. But it was nice having someone care for him.

"It doesn't matter what Jeffrey did or how he acted because I'm not him and you know that." Tommy stopped his gentle massage and tugged him back. "I'll understand if you just want to be friends. It's what we've been for nearly a decade, and that's okay if that's what you feel is right." He blinked, and Grayson caught Tommy's gaze.

"I've wanted or hoped to be more than friends for a while, but things never worked out, and when I finally got the guts to say something, you had met Xavier. I just don't want things to get messed up and funny if they don't work out." Grayson took a deep breath to quell the butterflies in his belly even as a wave of desire coursed through him. He wanted Tommy. He leaned closer until their lips met in a tentative kiss that grew more urgent and heated by the second. Grayson wound his arms around Tommy's waist, tugging him closer, deepening the kiss.

"Does that taste and feel like a bad idea?"

Grayson shook his head. It tasted like the start of a whole new world. "What about… you know…." He didn't want this to be a rebound thing.

"I don't know. It's over between us—you know that. I'd like to string Xavier up by his balls, but then, I don't want to have anything more to do with his balls, so how about we leave him three thousand miles away?"

That sounded like one hell of a good idea to him. At least things were good and done between them. He was still concerned about being a rebound guy, but the look in Tommy's eyes put a lot of that to rest.

Grayson stood deliberately and helped Tommy to his feet. Then Tommy tugged him toward the bedroom and closed the door behind them. The huge king-sized bed with white linens and cover called to them. Grayson flipped off the light, leaving the curtains open on the sea side, bathing the room in light from the stars and moon. "I think we might have waited too long for this," Grayson said as he pressed Tommy down on the bed.

"Why?" Tommy asked with a lilt to his voice.

"Because I want to open you up like a present on Christmas morning, and once I get to play with you, I'm probably not going to want to give you back." Grayson leaned over Tommy, tasting his swollen lips, even as he tugged at the hem of his shirt. If it had been one of those old, ratty things Tommy sometimes wore, he probably would have ripped it off him in his haste, but he got it over Tommy's head and tossed it to the side, not caring where it ended up. He was too far gone to pay attention to insignificant things like that.

Tommy's bare chest called to him, and Grayson took in every inch, from the lean, narrow hips to the soft lines on his belly.

"I know I'm not hot like you."

Grayson smiled. "You think I'm hot?"

Tommy wound his arms around Grayson's neck. "Smoking." He tugged Grayson to him. "I think you're the hottest guy I've seen in a long time. So how about you take off those clothes and show me what you got?" Tommy grinned wickedly.

"You've seen me naked before."

Tommy nodded and drew him close enough that Grayson could feel Tommy's breath on his ear. "Yes. But I wasn't allowed to touch before. I am now."

Grayson backed away, pulling off his shirt and kicking off his shoes.

"This isn't a race," Tommy chuckled even as he got his shoes off, and Grayson pulled off his socks.

"No, it isn't." Grayson stalked closer. "This is like my birthday, and you're the present I get to open." He popped the button on the waistband of Tommy's shorts and tugged them off, adding them to the pile of clothes on the floor. Then he leaned closer to suck at the base of Tommy's neck until he moaned softly.

Tommy tasted like heady male, spiced with salt and sea, a deadly attractive combination. God, Grayson groaned to himself as he slid lower, sucking a trail to one of Tommy's pink nipples, then teasing it with his tongue until the bud grew hard and Tommy shivered under him. He loved that he could make Tommy react like that. In his opinion there was nothing more attractive than a partner's erotic reaction.

Grayson pushed Tommy back down onto the mattress and held his hands still as he licked down his belly, tickling and teasing as he went, muscles fluttering under his lips. As he approached the waistband of Tommy's black briefs, he teased at it with his fingers, sliding them just underneath. Tommy stilled, and Grayson knew Tommy was waiting to see what he was going to do.

"Stop teasing," Tommy whispered.

"I'm not teasing." Grayson leaned closer, inhaling Tommy's musky scent before burying his nose in the growing bulge in those briefs. Now he was teasing, and, damn, Tommy whimpered as he ran his hands through Grayson's hair, adding pressure, wanting and needy.

Tommy's legs lay open, and Grayson ran his lips over Tommy's cotton-clad erection. At the head, he sucked it a little, sending Tommy into groans of passion.

"You're trying to kill me."

Grayson reached for the waistband and pulled it lower until Tommy's cock jumped free. Grayson tugged them down Tommy's legs, dropped them, and then ran his hand up Tommy's calves and over his thighs, getting closer and closer to his target, which bounced against Tommy's belly. Grayson slid his hands over Tommy's hips and belly, moving until he rested on top of him, kissing Tommy hard.

"You're mean, you know that," Tommy scolded once they broke the kiss. He shimmied off the bed, rolled Grayson on the mattress, and stalked back onto the bed. He yanked at Grayson's pants until he got them off, along with his boxers. "See, this is how you drive another man insane." Tommy leaned forward and sucked him between his lips.

Grayson gasped as his breath zoomed from his lungs and his head spun in near complete amazement. Tommy was talented, and dammit all to hell, when Grayson tried to regain his breath, Tommy just stole it all over again.

Tommy's wet heat drove him crazy, sending waves of passion the likes of which he had never felt before rushing through him. And to think he was worried about their friendship. Hell, if he'd have known Tommy was so uninhibited, he'd have approached him years ago.

Grayson stretched and groaned, letting Tommy have his way. There was nothing else he could do but grip the bedding and hold on for dear life as Tommy drove him completely wild. Grayson's legs throbbed, and he rocked them slightly on the bed. The energy and passion had to go somewhere, because if he tried to hold it in, he was going to explode. Tommy's lips sank down him and then tugged upward, making him shake with each movement.

"You... it's too soon," Grayson warned. He didn't want things to be over so quickly, but the combination of Tommy and what he was doing to him was more than his control was going to withstand. Thankfully, Tommy backed away, and Grayson tugged him upward, then stroked Tommy's back and down to his small butt.

Tommy sniffed slightly, and Grayson caressed his cheeks with his thumb. "What's going on?"

"I had no idea." Tommy hugged him tight. "You've been my friend all these years and I could have had you in my life... like this. I could have been with you and...."

"Sometimes it takes something out of the ordinary to see what's been right in front of us the whole time." Grayson couldn't help a smile. "I know you were always here." He stroked. "And to think I've been admiring your backside all this time."

Tommy snickered at him. "Is that all you want me for... my backside?"

"It is your best ass-et," Grayson countered, and Tommy groaned.

"You really need to work on that sense of humor of yours too. Maybe I should start making a list." Tommy waggled his eyebrows, and Grayson chuckled. God, it felt good to laugh and just enjoy. Sex was supposed to be joyful, happy, and easy.

"As long as I get to keep a list too."

Tommy grinned. "You can keep one of my ass-ets, if you want." He wriggled his hips, and Grayson groaned softly into Tommy's ear. God, this man was incredible. He leaned his head forward so he could kiss

Tommy, holding his smooth buttcheeks in his hands. He pressed them closer together, flexing his hips.

"I want you," Tommy whispered into Grayson's ear.

"I don't have anything." Grayson hadn't come on this trip expecting to go to bed with Tommy. He'd expected to have a good time, helping Tommy to get back on his emotional feet and to try to forget about Xavier. It seemed he was doing all of those things, just not in the way he'd originally expected.

Tommy giggled and climbed off him.

Grayson turned onto his side, gaze plastered to Tommy's adorable butt as he rummaged in his luggage. "I can understand needing lube for your honeymoon, but don't tell me you brought condoms."

Tommy turned to look at Grayson as though he were completely stupid. "Of course I did." He held up a strip with a smile.

Grayson swallowed hard, wondering just what Tommy was getting at. "You and Xavier never moved past using condoms?" Something was definitely afoul in Denmark. "Why not? You were going to marry him."

"Well, I've always used them, and Xavier never complained. I figured we'd talk about it when we were here, and I had hoped we could stop using them." The smile fell from his face. "Do you think that means he was seeing someone else or something?"

"No. But I think it was maybe another red flag about him." Grayson sat up, crooking his finger to get Tommy closer. "Anyway, that's a good thing with the way things turned out. You don't have to worry that he might have been seeing someone else and brought something home." Just another reason to gut the slimy pig as far as Grayson was concerned.

"We don't have to talk about him anymore, do we?" Tommy asked. "At least not while we're in my bedroom, naked. There are so many other things we could use our mouths for and they have nothing to do with that jerkwad."

Grayson lunged, grabbing Tommy around the waist, and pulled him toward the bed. "You got it." He maneuvered Tommy onto his back, figuring a much better use of his mouth was to make Tommy moan, so he sucked a path down his side to his cock, slid the crown over his tongue, and closed his lips around the shaft, sucking Tommy deep. It worked like a charm, and for the longest time, the only sounds that filled the room were those of abject passion.

Tommy whimpered softly, waving the line of condoms, though Grayson wasn't sure if he was aware that he still had them in his hands. The damn packages were red, like waving a cape in front of a bull. Grayson snatched them, tore one off, and ripped the package open with his teeth. He pulled back to roll one down his length. Keeping one hand on Tommy's belly to maintain contact, he searched for the damn lube, snatched the bottle, and hastily prepared both Tommy and himself.

This wasn't going to last long. His legs shook with pent-up energy. "I don't want to hurt you," Grayson said, managing to keep the red of desire from clouding his judgment.

Tommy's eyes were glazed and his mouth hung open. He placed his hands on Grayson's shoulders, hips rocking forward. "Please," muttered plaintively, was all he said, in a tone that nearly snapped Grayson's control like a twig. He was holding on by a hair as he pressed forward. Tommy's body opened to him, volcano-like heat engulfing him.

Grayson leaned closer and took Tommy's lips in a kiss that threatened to flash-sear both of them. Sinking deeper, grip tightening, he bit his lower lip to keep from crying his ecstasy to the moon and stars outside. Damn, he wanted to let go completely, but he had to wait, to let Tommy find his pleasure. God, he wanted to see Tommy in the throes of release. That alone would be worth the years of waiting, watching, dreaming, and wondering.

"Grayson." Tommy tugged him closer. "I think I've been waiting just as long as you have."

Grayson's release barely remained at bay as Tommy moved with him. When Tommy let go of his shoulders, Grayson leaned back just enough to give Tommy room, and then seconds later, the pressure around him increased, Tommy's breathing becoming more urgent. Then everything stopped as Tommy shook under him. The moon provided just enough light to see the glow in Tommy's eyes as his passion crested, then built before breaking over both of them, shattering the last of Grayson's control… and he flew.

He came back to himself as Tommy stroked his cheek. Grayson blinked and pulled Tommy to him. He didn't want to move, because moving meant disconnection, the world intruding, and for these few seconds, it was only him and Tommy. No one else mattered, the universe held at blissful bay.

Seconds stretched to minutes, everything outside their bubble not leaving them alone, pushing back. Grayson groaned and pulled away, kisses now gentle, the passion spent. He backed off the bed and half floated to the bathroom, then returned with a towel and gently cleaned his lover, his best friend, taking care of him. Tommy was special. He already had his heart if he wanted it, and Grayson wanted Tommy to know he was cherished. Throwing the towel back into the bathroom, he wondered if he should go to his room, but Tommy was already climbing under the covers, and Grayson got between the sheets and held Tommy as the sound of the sea outside lulled them both to sleep.

Chapter Five

TOMMY was dreaming—he had to be. That was the only explanation. He shifted as a soft snore rumbled in his ears. Then he remembered. He wasn't dreaming; Grayson was in bed with him. Light streamed in the window, waves lapped on the beach, the cry of birds outside, the rumble of a boat motor, someone pounding on their door. He shook his head, pushing back the covers.

"Make them go away," Grayson muttered.

"Did you order breakfast?" Tommy asked. "You're in my bed. Oh God. What about Petey?"

Grayson stretched and smiled as the pounding started again. "I have permission, remember?"

Tommy grabbed his robe, and the pounding stopped.

"What are you doing here?" Petey asked loudly. "Go away. You suck and we don't want you."

Slam. The walls of the bungalow vibrated.

Grayson was out of bed instantly, grabbing his clothes. He pulled on a pair of shorts, and Tommy yanked open the door to find Petey by the front door, glaring at it. "Who was that?"

"Xavier. I told him to go away." Petey hurried over to Grayson when he stepped out of the room.

"That wasn't all you said," Grayson clarified.

"Nope. But I didn't lie. I told the truth." Petey's hands went to his hips, and he looked about as indignant as any nine-year-old could. "I don't want him here and he sucks." He motioned for Grayson to come closer, and Grayson slid an arm around him.

"Tommy." Xavier stood on the dock outside the screen door.

"Can't take a hint, can you," Tommy said as he walked over to the man who'd left him on their wedding day, leaving the screen between them.

"We need to talk," Xavier said.

"No. You need to go away before I call the resort and have you removed." Tommy crossed his arms over his chest as the war inside him started. He'd been fine as long as Grayson was here and Xavier was gone. It was easy to hate the guy when he wasn't there to defend himself, but standing in front of him, Tommy felt some of the anger slipping away, and it worried him.

"Tommy, I'm sorry for what happened, but we really need to talk."

"No. Go away, scumbag." Petey walked to the patio door and shut it. Then he locked it and tugged the curtains closed.

Damn, it was nice to have support.

"Thank you."

"He's a jerk." Petey walked past them into his room. "Can we eat now? I'm hungry."

Tommy's mind tried to process how quickly Petey's thoughts could switch from topic to topic.

"Go on and get dressed," Grayson told him as Xavier knocked on the bungalow door once again.

"I know you can hear me, Tommy."

He groaned. Tommy just wanted him to go the hell away. He was finally starting to feel better and was happy, or at least he'd found out that he could be happy with someone... and Xavier wasn't him. Now all he wanted was the time to figure things out. And dammit all, it looked like he wasn't going to get it.

Tommy opened the door. "Don't come in," he said before anything else.

"You want to talk here?" Xavier said, crossing his tanned arms over his powerful chest.

"I don't want to talk to you at all. I want you to turn around and go home. I will call security and have you removed. I mean it." He had already had enough of Xavier to last him the rest of his life. "You left me standing in the chapel with all my friends and family, and...." Tommy balled his hands into fists. "So help me, you need to leave me the hell alone and go away."

"I need somewhere to stay...." He pushed out his lower lip, and Tommy wanted to grab the thing and rip it off his face. That sure as hell wasn't going to work.

"Stay on the beach or crawl under a rock somewhere, but you aren't setting foot in here. I'm trying to move on from the mess you made."

"The resort is full. I tried the ones in the area as well, and they're all booked up."

"So what? Poor planning on your part doesn't mean shit to me. I don't care what happens to you. But you have ten seconds to be gone and off this property before I call the main desk and have you removed."

Grayson came up behind him and placed a hand on his shoulder. "I already called, and they're sending someone over to take out the trash." Grayson squeezed lightly, and Tommy leaned back a bit.

"I get it," Xavier leered. "You two... with a kid. What are you doing now, Tommy, playing house?" He stepped closer, and Tommy wanted to hit him. He'd never been a violent man, but more than anything he wanted to kick Xavier's ass into the middle of next week.

"Is there a problem?" a huge man asked from behind Xavier. He had to be six four, towering over Tommy.

"Yes. This man is bothering us and he isn't staying at the resort. I'm not sure how he got in here, but he needs to leave. Could you please escort him off the property?" Tommy met the security guard's eyes. "Also, please inform the resort staff that he is not be allowed to stay at the resort. That would cause problems for us." Tommy grinned at Xavier, who was seething. It had clearly been his plan to try to see if there was any space available or a last-minute cancellation.

"Of course, sir," the guard said, turning to Xavier. "The exit is this way." He motioned to Xavier, who looked like he was going to have steam coming out of his ears at any moment.

"Thank you," Tommy told the guard and closed the door. "Son of a bitch. He had to show up here."

"Why?" Grayson asked. "What is he doing here and what does he want?"

Tommy shook his head. "I need to check my accounts to make sure there aren't any charges that shouldn't be there." Xavier was an assistant to an interior designer in Milwaukee. He didn't have the money to fly down here on a whim, and the ticket that Tommy had bought for him had been turned in. So where had the money for this jaunt come from?

"You do that." Grayson went to the bedroom he shared with Petey, and Tommy went to his own, got dressed, and then used his computer to check the accounts for any charges. He didn't see any pending and was somewhat relieved.

As he closed his computer, Tommy wondered why this had to happen now, turning to stare at the bed he and Grayson had messed up so completely and amazingly. He could still feel some of the aftereffects of their activities from last night. Now everything was messed up. Xavier was here, and…. He sat on the edge of the bed, trying to figure out what he was going to do.

A soft knock on the door interrupted his thoughts. Grayson came in and gathered up his clothes from last night. "You did a great job handling him."

"Thanks. But what happens now? Am I going to have to stay here on the resort in order to keep from seeing him everywhere we go? How the hell did he get here anyway?" The trip had been going so well so far. Tommy hadn't been thinking about his idiot ex, and now here he was on this small island and there weren't many places he could go to stay away from him.

"No. You're going to do the things we planned and have fun. That's what you came here for, and we're going to do it. After all, we have Petey, and he's obviously not shy about telling Xavier what he thinks of him." Grayson smiled, and Tommy tried to stop the chuckle that bubbled up from inside.

"I do wish I could have seen him slamming the door in his face. That would be a sight. But I did love the way he closed the patio door and pulled the curtains. That kid is something else."

"Dad, Uncle Tommy," Petey called, shuffling into the room. "Can we eat now? I'm really hungry."

"Finish getting dressed and we'll go," Grayson said, but Petey didn't move. "What is it?"

"Are you going to stay in here with Uncle Tommy for the rest of the trip?"

Tommy tried to check to see if that was upsetting for Petey or not. He had heard the remarks about the horizontal hula, but being funny was different from actually being around his dad sleeping with someone else. "He can. But if you'd feel better… it's whatever you want."

Petey nodded. "Then he can sleep in here. He snores." He did a pretty accurate impression of the sounds Grayson made at night before racing away.

"You two eat when the food gets here. I'm going to try to work for a while." Tommy felt the need to get away and retreat. He lifted his gaze and saw Grayson was about to argue with him. "Just let me wrap my head around all this."

"All right. Breakfast will be here any minute, but we need to meet for snuba in an hour." The growl in his voice killed the protest on Tommy's lips.

Tommy didn't think he was going to be very good company. He wanted to sit in the room, work, and try to hide from all this drama. "I'll be okay. I promise." He stood but jumped a little at the knock on the front door. Grayson went to answer it, and Tommy took a few minutes in the bathroom to splash some water on his face. Then he got dressed for the day and decided to join the two of them at the table.

He was pretty proud of himself when he sat down. Tommy didn't eat much, his appetite from the day before long gone. He nibbled on a muffin and drank some coffee, trying to ignore the fact that Grayson kept sneaking goodies onto his plate.

"This is gonna be fun."

"What is snuba?" Tommy asked as he drank the last of his coffee and poured himself some more.

"It's like scuba but with a partner and a floating tank. All you do is use the mask and breathe. There's a line to the boat for air, but a guide is with you for safety. The website says that there's some instruction that's given first, but mostly you kick back and see the world under the water."

"How many people do they do at once?" Tommy asked.

"Two. So I thought you could go with Petey and I'd go by myself."

Tommy wasn't sure about this, but the snorkeling had gone amazingly well and he'd had a great time, so this could be really fun. He expected that if he got weirded out, they'd take him to the surface right away.

"You're not sure about this, are you?" Grayson said.

"Uncle Tommy, it's going to be so cool. We'll be able to see things up close, and there could even be more turtles and sea horses. The man by the pool yesterday said that when he went, they saw really big fish." Petey held his arms apart.

"You don't have to go if you really don't want to." Grayson scooted his chair closer. "But I know you'll sit here and worry about Xavier and what he's up to. Come with us at least. If you don't want to go under the water, you can stay on the boat." He turned to Petey, who looked so hopeful, there was no way Tommy could say no.

"Okay. Let's finish eating and we can go. Where do we have to meet?"

"The information sheet says they'll pick us up at our dock." Grayson checked his watch. "So at least we won't have to worry about seeing Xavier somewhere in town."

Tommy nodded. Just when he thought he was getting his legs under him, something happened to knock them away. "I'll be fine." The urge to retreat behind his work surfaced again, but he was determined not to do that. Petey was really excited, and so was Grayson, so Tommy was not going to let them down. It was reassuring that both of them had his back.

Tommy hurried to get ready and then sat down to work for a few minutes and have some quiet time.

"It looks like the boat is coming," Petey called, having pulled open the curtains and the sliding door.

"Stay inside until Tommy and I are with you," Grayson said, repeating the rules. Tommy saw him grab a bag that he hadn't seen him pack. "I've got everything we need."

Tommy opened the screen and walked out on the dock with Petey, who ran ahead, looking at everything in the water. "Our boat's gone," Petey said.

"Yes. We weren't going to use it as much as I thought. The resort is going to let others have it, and all we have to do is call and they'll bring it back when we want to take a ride." Tommy patted his pack as a medium-sized sailboat glided up to the dock.

"Ahoy there."

"Johan, you really do everything here, don't you?" Tommy stood back while Johan tied off the boat. Grayson joined them, and they embarked for their trip. "Is it only us?"

"There's another couple, and they'll be here in just a minute." Johan got them settled as a man and a woman, both about forty, strode between the bungalows and down the dock. They got on and settled. "This is your crew: Franklin and Gregor, and I'm Johan. If anyone needs anything, just holler. We're going to motor away from the dock a little ways, put up the sail, and then head out to an underwater reef. This one is deeper than those at Klein Bonaire. We'll dive there. So sit back and relax."

Tommy took a seat, and Petey and Grayson sat on either side of him. He did his best to relax but found he kept looking around, expecting to see Xavier at any second. What had been carefree and wonderful had now turned into worry and uncertainty.

"It's okay, Uncle Tommy. This is going to be fun. I always wanted to go diving." Petey leaned forward. "Maybe next time I can take lessons. Right, Dad?"

Tommy broke in before Grayson could answer. "If we come to a place like this again, then you and your dad can take scuba lessons." Tommy would do just about anything to put that kind of excited smile on Petey's face. His eyes shone and his butt barely stayed on the seat, he was so antsy with anticipation.

"You too…," Petey said. "If Dad and I do it, then you have to too."

Grayson patted Petey's leg. "Why don't you settle down a little? We'll see if we like it, and then we can plan possible future lessons." Grayson was always so practical.

The crew put up the sails, and Johan turned off the engine. The boat glided over the water. Now this was the life. Tommy had liked when they'd gone out in the speed boat, but this was amazing. Sheer quiet, with just the air rushing around him. Finally some of the stress from Xavier's reappearance leached away. How could anyone be out on the water like this, just the boat, you, and the wind, and not feel at one with nature?

"Have you ever done anything like this before?" Johan asked them.

"No," Grayson answered. "We snorkeled yesterday, which you helped us arrange, but other than that, no."

"All right. We'll anchor the boat, and each of you will be partnered with one of our three guides. We limit this excursion to six people so that each of you has enough time under water. You'll dive three at a time. You'll breathe through a regulator that's attached up here at the boat, and one of our divers will be with each of you the entire time. It's a combination of snorkeling and scuba."

"Cool."

"Each of you will be down for half an hour. Fred and Shirley have done this before, so I thought we'd let them go first so you all can see how it's done."

"Good idea."

"It's really easy," the woman said from the other seat across from them. "Fred and I did this on Aruba a few years ago. It was great, and we got to get close to a shipwreck. The important thing is to breathe normally and just enjoy the scenery."

"Are there any sea turtles?" Petey asked. "I saw some yesterday, and I want to see a big one and maybe a shark."

"You never know. Though we don't get big sharks here most of the time. As I said, each of the divers is here for your safety and to make sure you have an experience to remember." Johan took his place behind the wheel once again, and the other guys began passing out equipment and checking that everything fit.

Once they anchored the boat, the crew got suited up and ready. Then two of them took Shirley and Fred on their dive from opposite sides of the boat. Petey kept his eyes glued to the water, watching as the divers moved around below.

"It's amazing how deep you can see," Tommy remarked.

Grayson nodded, holding on to Petey so he didn't go over the side in his excitement.

"I can't wait, Dad."

"You'll have to. Just be patient, because when you're underwater, you need to be able to think and do things right. So settle down." It was clear that Grayson was a little worried about Petey being under the water.

"Franklin is staying up here during your dive, and I'm going to be partnered with Petey here," Johan explained. "He and I are going to have a good time. Aren't we?" He ushered Petey away to get him ready, and Grayson took Tommy's hand, lacing their fingers together.

"Petey and I can go down, and you can stay here if you like. I know you're not a water baby the way he is. Petey is so excited, he isn't going to miss that you aren't down there with us." He squeezed Tommy's fingers.

"I want to go—I'm just not a very good swimmer, and I don't want to get in trouble." This activity was one thing that was not and would never be on his bucket list. "Or ruin everyone else's fun."

"You won't. I promise. Besides, this is about you having fun, and I think that you've done amazingly well so far on this trip. You snorkeled and had a good time. You've gone in the pool and things. If this is too much, just stay here with the guys, drink some rum punch, and enjoy the scenery."

Tommy nodded. The truth was, being under the water like that scared the hell out of him. "Then I'll stay here and watch the two of you." He was so relieved, it was hard for him to put into words. As the time got closer for them to dive, his belly had begun cramping and his ears rang. Instantly all that ended and he was happy and semirelaxed once again.

Shirley and Fred came up, all smiles, and Petey and Grayson prepared to go down. Tommy pulled out his phone and snapped pictures as they went into the water, then watched as they moved around beneath the waves.

"Decided not to go?" Fred asked.

"I don't swim well, and this was really for Petey. He's completely sea turtle obsessed. We saw some yesterday when we went snorkeling, and he hasn't stopped talking about it since."

Franklin asked about drinks, and Tommy took Grayson's advice and ordered a rum punch that he drank down in a few gulps. It was fruity, sweet, and perfect on a hot, sunny day. He got another and then switched to just fruit juice, nursing it to pass the time until Grayson and Petey returned.

"It was awesome! I got really close to the big fish," Petey said, hurrying over once he was on deck and had gotten out of his gear. "They stared at me and I stared right back." He grinned as Tommy got the bag and pulled out a towel for him.

"Did you see your turtles?"

"No. But there was a shark. It was only this big"— he held his hands apart—"and it stayed away, but it was cool." Petey sat down, and Tommy made sure he got dried off before helping him into his T-shirt.

Grayson joined them, and Tommy handed him a towel as well. He couldn't help noticing where Grayson's suit was a little clingy, especially since the clingy bits were at eye level. Tommy passed Grayson his shirt as they pulled up anchor. The crew passed out sandwiches and fruit, as well as drinks, then hoisted the sail for their trip back to the resort.

"I'm sorry you didn't go," Petey told him. "I know you don't really like the water and stuff."

"Diving can be something you do with your dad." Tommy accepted the glass of fruit punch and sat back. "When I was growing up, my dad and I both liked baseball. He and I used to go to a couple of Brewers games each year. It was something he and I did together. Dad would buy the tickets, and we'd go, watch the game, and eat hot dogs and popcorn until I was ready to get sick. Eventually we got too busy and didn't go anymore. I think that was because I grew up."

"I'd go with you to watch baseball."

"Maybe we could all ask my dad to go with us." Tommy grinned. "But I told you that because sometimes it's important to have things you do just with your dad." Just like there were things that only he and Grayson would do. He caught Grayson's gaze and winked. "And there will be things that you and I do. Like video games, maybe."

"What kinds of things did you do with your mom?" Petey scooted closer, scratching his head. "Mine is coming back from Africa at the end of the summer."

"My mother and I used to bake cookies. In fact, I bet if you asked her, she'd teach you how to bake cookies, and then you could show your mom when she comes home." Anne was not the kind of person to bake anything, but Tommy remembered her as a good sport.

They cut through the water under sail, and Petey made his way up front to lie in the netting between the catamaran hulls so he could watch the water rush under them.

"Just be careful," Grayson cautioned and didn't relax until Petey was settled. "Some days I swear he's going to give me gray hair. He's always so active and has tons of energy…." He sighed. "His teacher at school suggested I look into getting him on something for hyperactivity. She says he can be disruptive sometimes."

"Don't," Tommy said. "He's got a lot of energy, but he can focus too. Did you discuss it with the doctor?"

"Not yet. I was going to wait until summer and then see what happens. I did a classroom visit, and Petey was just fine. The other kids seem to like him, and the only time I saw him get fidgety was when he was bored. So I'm also looking into more advanced placement for him to keep him engaged." They both turned to watch Petey, who lay still, watching everything around him.

"He doesn't miss much of anything, and you can see him taking it all in. I'd hate to put him on something he doesn't really need."

"Me too. I did talk to the teacher and ask her to challenge him more, but I don't think I got anywhere."

"You have to go up the ladder. Get an advocate and make them listen." Tommy felt the urgency growing inside him. "They have so many students that if you don't push and make them listen, nothing will happen." He pursed his lips. "I was different in school. I bet you can guess that. I was smart, I know that now, but everything went so slowly, so I acted up because I had nothing to do. They gave me assignments the other kids worked through for an hour and I was done in minutes, or I didn't do it at all because I already knew it and it seemed stupid to me. The teachers went to my mom and said I needed pills because I was hyperactive. She listened to them, and the doctor prescribed them. Of course, the kids at school found out and they called me names, and I did less work and got angrier and acted out even more."

"You?" Grayson put an arm around Tommy, and he leaned into the care it represented. "I don't get it."

"I was a terror. But my mom didn't give up. I remember her coming into the school, charging up the walk and into the principal's office. She was angry, and I thought I was in trouble… as usual." He could see his mother coming toward the building like a lion out for blood. "I didn't know it, but those tests they gave us in school… well, Mom got the results and she was furious because they said I was supersmart. Mom made the school put together some sort of plan, and I got tested again, and then they gave me more work and I did better. I also got glasses."

Grayson chuckled. "You with glasses? I bet you were really cute." He bumped him on the shoulder.

"I don't know about that, and thankfully I didn't have to wear them forever. There was something wrong with my eyes that could be corrected, so I wore the glasses for a year, and things at school really changed. I became a good student. But it was because my mom fought for me. Petey can't fight for himself."

"Would you go? I can be the strong one, but you're the smart one." A nervous Grayson wasn't something he was used to. He was confident and sure of himself so much of the time that it threw Tommy for a second. But then he smiled. Grayson wanted him to go with him—he wanted Tommy's help.

"We'll be back at the dock in about twenty minutes," Franklin explained as he passed a tray of sandwiches. "Can I get you anything more to drink?"

They were both good, but Grayson got some more juice for Petey and called him over. He drank it and sat next to Tommy, excitement rolling off him. It was so wonderful to see Petey so happy. Hell, Tommy was happy.

He put his arm around Petey, pulling him closer. "What do you want to have for dinner?"

Petey thought for a second. "Can we have pizza?"

Tommy grinned and then laughed. "Somehow I don't think they have the kind of pizza you're expecting. How about we have something else, and I promise that when we get home I'll get you all the pizza you can eat." Tommy patted Petey's belly. "I'm starting to think this thing never gets full."

Petey looked down. "It doesn't, I guess." He lifted his gaze. "Is that bad?"

"Nope." Tommy's grin grew. "You're a growing boy and need plenty of food to keep growing." He sat back, lifting his gaze to the scenery, letting contentment wash through him.

"Are you still sad about what happened with jerkface?" Petey asked.

Tommy shrugged. He was really beginning to think that Xavier had done him a favor.

"Uncle Tommy, look…." Petey pointed toward the dock. "It's the jerkface and he's waiting for us."

"Petey, we don't talk like that," Grayson said as he turned. "Even if he is a jerkface." He winked, trying to lighten the mood, but as they got closer to the dock, Tommy saw that Petey was right. Xavier stood on the end in a pair of tan shorts and blue T-shirt, his arms crossed over his chest, even though he'd been told to stay off the resort. Tommy could most definitely have gone the rest of his life without seeing him again.

"You want me to take care of him?" Grayson asked. "I'll get the resort staff to remove him again."

Tommy sighed. "He's only going to stay here and be a pain in the ass until I talk to him." The thought made his stomach churn. He'd only wanted to spend the week to try to get over what happened, and it seemed that Xavier wasn't going to allow him that. Why couldn't Tommy have seen just how selfish and thoughtless Xavier was before he'd asked him to marry him?

"I don't think that's a good idea. But you're probably right. Do you want me with you when you talk to him?"

He should have known Grayson would be there if he needed him. Grayson had always been there for him.

"No." This was something he needed to do on his own.

Tommy took a deep breath as the sails were lowered. The crew packed it away, and Johan started the engine, breaking the quiet just as much as Xavier had shattered the contentment that had begun to settle over Tommy.

They docked, and Tommy thanked the guys, got off the boat, and approached Xavier.

"You and I really need to talk."

Tommy stepped off to the side. Grayson patted him on the shoulder as he passed and took Petey inside. "You can't leave me alone? You hurt me badly, and now when I'm trying to move on, you come here and…." He turned to Xavier, not looking him in the eye. "So what's so damned important that you have to come here and bother me? You have to know that I don't want to see you at all for any reason."

Petey came back out, hurrying to stand next to him. "What do you want, jerkface? Can't you leave him alone?"

Tommy put his arm around Petey's shoulders. "Say what you wanted to say and then go. And I don't want to see you again, ever." He'd had quite enough of all of this.

That seemed to rattle Xavier for a second. "It seems your aunt filed suit on your behalf, suing me for the cost of the wedding."

Tommy nodded slowly. "I think that sounds more than fair, especially since you left me standing there alone, and I went through all that trouble and expense when you had no intention of marrying me. I loved you, and you treated me like crap. So whatever Aunt Ginny has planned for you, I say you deserve it. If that's all you came for, to try to get me to drop it, you wasted a trip and money you'll need for other things." He was quickly growing to hate Xavier. "Come on, Petey. Let's go inside." He took a few steps toward the bungalow.

"Do you think I'm that dumb? That I came here unarmed?"

Tommy tensed. He had no idea what the comment meant, but his reaction was visceral. He pushed Petey behind him, half expecting to turn to find himself looking down the barrel of a gun. "What are you talking about?" he asked, keeping Petey behind him for safety.

"It seems that you drew up papers to have me added to your house. Which I thought very nice of you. Especially since I have a copy of the paperwork." Xavier pulled a piece of paper out of his pocket and handed it to him.

"Those were destroyed when you walked out on me." He checked it over and ripped the copy to shreds. "You have nothing to stand on. I canceled the deal, and the papers were never filed."

Xavier stepped closer. "That was only a copy. It seems all of the copies weren't destroyed. So you better figure out what you're going to do because I'm going to want half the house. I'm entitled to it, and I have the paperwork to back me up."

Tommy felt cold. That house, his home, was his refuge. Yes, he had intended to add Xavier to it, but not any longer. He should have listened to his aunt and waited, but he had been holding the papers as a wedding present. His hands clenched to fists. "Just go. I'm not giving you anything, including half the house."

"Oh, I'll go." Xavier turned his lips up into a sneer. "But this isn't going to go away. I figure I'll go to court and ask for half the house, and with the paperwork I have, I'm sure I can make you pay." He scoffed and turned to walk away.

Petey raced around Tommy. "Stop being a jerk." He ran into Xavier, who stumbled, then tried to steady himself, but there was no more dock and he fell into the water with a splash.

Tommy peered over the side, and when he saw Xavier stand up and heard the swearing, he turned away again. "Come on. I've had enough of his drama." He led Petey inside the bungalow, then closed and locked the sliding door. He found Grayson on the sofa, felt him watching as he went to his bedroom, shut the door, and lay down on the bed, pulling his knees to his chest. He hated this and knew he should just deal with it. But Xavier was trying to take away his home, or part of his home. Tommy closed his eyes and breathed deeply, waiting for the panic attack to pass. God, he'd made it through being left at the altar without having one. He thought he was done with them, but here it was.

"Tommy," Grayson said. "Hey, what's this?" The side of the bed dipped. "Petey told me what Xavier said. You know he's completely full of shit."

"How do you know? He's trying to take away my house."

"No. He's trying to use the threat to get to you." Grayson rubbed his back gently. "That's what he's doing. What does he really want from you?" Grayson was so gentle and his voice so caring, Tommy calmed ever so slightly.

"I guess Aunt Ginny filed suit because he left me at the altar." Tommy inhaled again, trying to bring the panic under control. He kept his eyes closed and willed his mind to get hold of itself. He and a doctor had worked to give him techniques so he could cope with extreme situations. "I would have thought what he did when he left me would have done this...."

"Hey," Grayson breathed, continuing to stroke his back. "You had everyone around you then, and Xavier wasn't there to try to push your buttons."

The door to the room opened and closed, and the other side of the bed dipped. "The jerkface is gone. I watched him through the curtains."

"I bet he looked like a drowned rat," Tommy said, patting Petey's hand, straightening out his legs. "You did real good. He needed to cool off, and hopefully a good soaking did him some good." He tried to clear his head. "He says he has papers... copies of the paperwork to put his name on the house."

"Call Aunt Ginny when you feel better. She will know exactly what to do."

"I could just ask her to drop the lawsuit." Tommy breathed deeply, the panic passing as he started to think once again.

"And what would he want next?" Grayson asked.

Tommy felt his stomach roiling again, and he so wanted to be alone so he could fall to pieces. But he wasn't going to do that in front of Grayson and Petey. He didn't want them to think he was crazy or something. "I don't know."

"Let's call Aunt Ginny and set her on it. She's the pit bull in your family. She'll know what to do."

Grayson reached for Tommy's phone and handed it to him. Tommy unlocked it, and Grayson took it back. The call must have gone to voicemail, and Grayson left a message and hung up.

"She'll call back." Tommy knew that, though he wished none of this was necessary. "We should get something to eat." He sat up and got off the bed. "I'm sorry for—"

"You feel bad, and he was a real douchebag."

"Petey, you won't talk that way. I don't care if it is true, you still shouldn't talk like that. It isn't proper, and your grandmother will have a fit if she hears that."

Petey shifted his gaze downward. "Yes, Dad."

Tommy put a hand on Petey's shoulder. "You know, I've found that dumb people swear and rant. Smart people can find the words to express themselves."

"Is that why you never swear and stuff?" Petey asked.

"Yup. I like to think I'm pretty smart, and I know you are. So why don't we make a deal? No swearing, and we don't need to call Xavier names." Tommy leaned closer. "Even if he is a douchebag." He squeezed Petey's hand and glanced at Grayson, who rolled his eyes. "Now, let's go get something to eat before you waste away to nothing." Not that Tommy was hungry. But if he didn't eat, then mother hen Grayson would start fussing.

Petey nodded and stood. "Are we gonna eat in the dining room?"

"Why don't we? Tomorrow I'll make a call and we can go out on the boat again." It wasn't likely Xavier was going to be able to interrupt anything then. Not with all the other resort guests around. Once he was able to talk to his aunt and get her on this paperwork stuff, he'd feel a whole lot better.

"Awesome." Petey hugged him and hurried out of the room.

Grayson came over, leaned down, and kissed him gently. "You're so good with Petey."

"Is that your way of telling me something?"

"You mean, that I love you? Nope. I'll just say that outright. I do love you, and so does Petey." Grayson grinned, and Tommy returned it.

Tommy had no doubt that was true, but he couldn't help wondering if things would be different when they returned to the real world. Here they were together all the time, and Tommy had put his work on hold in favor of fun in the sun. But would things work out once they got home and Tommy went back to his usual work schedule? He sure hoped so. "I love you too." He kept his doubts to himself. He needed to give this a chance and not nip it in the bud before anything had an opportunity to happen.

"Let's go on to dinner and get you fed." Grayson took his hand and walked to the door. "I know you're upset and that you don't have an appetite when that happens, but you need to eat something. If Xavier is going to be a pain, then you need to be strong enough to fend him off."

Tommy nodded and began getting ready for dinner.

Chapter Six

DINNER was nice, but Tommy didn't eat very much. Before they went back to the bungalow, Grayson made a stop at the sundry shop and got some chips, Cheetos, and a few Diet Cokes, knowing Tommy liked them. He was also able to get some fresh fruit that he hoped he could entice Tommy with.

He thought he might have seen Xavier as he strode through the resort and wondered why he was there, but if it was Xavier, he headed the other direction, and Grayson hurried back to the bungalow.

Petey and Tommy sat on the floor in front of the television, playing video games.

"How did you get that to work?"

"I tweaked the game and transferred it to the television. Now we can play on the bigger screen." Tommy

sat back and restarted the game, and then he and Petey
battled each other in a driving game. Grayson had never
been one for video games and didn't really understand his
son's fascination.

"Come play, Dad," Petey said.

"Yeah. Come play with us," Tommy echoed.

For a second Grayson wondered which of the two
of them was the bigger kid, before he sat on the floor
and Tommy explained how the game worked.

Of course, Petey beat him easily, and then Tommy
did the same. But Grayson began to get the hang of things,
and after that, he began to play better. He didn't have a
chance to actually win a game against either of those two,
but he did enjoy himself, even if his car ended up in flames
each and every time. What he considered a win was that
Tommy and Petey ate all the snacks and then Grayson said
good night to Petey, who put on his pajamas and came
back out to say good night to both of them, giving him
and Tommy a hug before going to his room. Petey didn't
close the door, and Grayson went through the living room,
turning out the lights. He'd been tempted to go outside
and even opened the door, but a shower had wetted down
everything so he closed it again, sitting next to Tommy on
the sofa in the dark room.

"I'm sorry for everything. It sucks, and it makes
me angry that he can't leave you alone."

"He's like the bad penny that keeps turning up, or
the mistake that I have to pay for over and over again.
And what sucks is that I didn't figure it all out. I loved
him, or at least I thought I did." Tommy leaned against
him. "I don't think I understood what it meant to love
someone then."

"It was only a week ago." Grayson turned toward
him, their gazes meeting.

"I know. But I know now what it feels like to love someone and be loved back. That was what was missing. Xavier didn't love me. He never looked at me like I was the most important man in the world. Hell, he looked at his friends with more fondness than he ever gave to me." Tommy swallowed hard.

"I don't understand."

Tommy held his hand, and Grayson felt it shaking. "Sometimes we'd go out with his friends, and they'd drink and have a good time. I always seemed on the outside of their conversations. There were jokes they all understood but I didn't, and Xavier never explained them to me. Of course, at the end of the evening, I was the one paying the tab because I wanted to be generous and wanted them to like me. Not that it did me any good at all." Tommy shook his head. "I was such a fool. Yeah, Xavier was a gold digger, and after a brief bout of conscience, he returned to form and is now trying to blackmail me."

"It isn't going to work. Aunt Ginny will find a way to stop him. He may have a copy of the paperwork, but you have witnesses who will testify that you didn't intend to go through with it in the end." Grayson needed to help Tommy calm down and relax. The agitation in his voice was only growing more acute. This whole thing was weighing on him, and every time Grayson hoped he had Tommy calmed down, Xavier would make an appearance and stir the pot once again. Somehow Grayson needed to put an end to that. "Let me make sure all the doors are closed and locked, and then we'll go to bed."

Tommy nodded in the darkness. "It's pretty obvious that Petey is asleep and isn't expecting you to sleep in the room with him tonight."

"No. Petey is very happy to have the room to himself." Grayson could see very little, especially with the curtains drawn, but then, he didn't need to. He knew where Tommy was and simply closed his eyes and followed his earthy scent to get closer.

"Petey is right about one thing. You do snore." Tommy chuckled, and Grayson gathered him into his arms, holding him. Tommy was too nerved up, almost rigid and shaking. Grayson stroked his back like he'd done earlier and let him work things through. Grayson was aware that he could try to make all the arguments in the world about why Tommy shouldn't worry, but he was going to anyhow. He wondered if he should try to make Tommy forget. He knew how to do that.

"Come on." Grayson got up and tugged Tommy to his feet, then walked with him, hand in hand, to his bedroom and quietly closed the door. "Go on and take a shower. I'll be there in a few minutes."

He waited for Tommy to go in the bathroom. Then Grayson went over to his and Petey's room and grabbed some clothes, making sure he didn't wake Petey. When he returned to Tommy's room, the bathroom door was shut and the shower was running. Grayson stripped and opened the door to step inside. He closed the door, pushed open the back of the shower curtain, and slid into the shower behind Tommy.

"I don't think I'm up for anything… tonight." Tommy sounded miserable.

"It's okay." Grayson reached for the soap, lathered his hands, and soaped up Tommy's back. "Just relax and stop worrying about what everyone else wants. It's okay to take what *you* need every once in a while." He washed Tommy's back and then his shoulders, stroking, soaping, taking care and showing concern.

"But… I mean, this is our second night, and after last night, I'd thought you…."

"You thought that everything would be perfect and that we'd make love every night? And since we can't, you think I'm going to be angry, or disappointed?" Grayson pressed his chest to Tommy's back. "Making love is something we do together. It isn't something we do because we're supposed to. So don't worry about it if you aren't up for it." He slid his hands around to Tommy's belly. "Though I do think you're super sexy."

"Me?" Tommy slowly turned around, and Grayson let his hands slide along as he did. "I've never been sexy, and I doubt I ever will be. You know those guys who turn gray around the temples and just get hotter than hell? That isn't going to be me. I'm going to get old, and everything is—"

Grayson cut Tommy off with a kiss. "Sexy is in the eye of the beholder." He held Tommy to him, kissing him hard, demanding, his passion rising. "Feel what you do to me?"

Tommy nodded slowly, and Grayson kissed harder. His intent wasn't sex, but to get the message through Tommy's worry that he was cared for and that Grayson wanted more than sex. He pulled back and reached for the soap again, ignoring his own erection as he lathered his hands and soaped Tommy's chest.

"Just close your eyes." He washed his chest and down his belly. Tommy was excited as well, but that faded for both of them once the idea sank into their heads that this was an exercise in intimacy. There was something special, warm and close, about being together, naked, touching without the need for sex. He reached for the shampoo, washed Tommy's hair, and then guided him under the water, sluicing away the soap and hopefully some of Tommy's anxiety.

Tommy swung his head, shaking some of the water out of his hair, then lathered his hands to soap Grayson's chest. His excitement returned, but Grayson ignored it as best he could. It was difficult, and he grew harder the longer Tommy's almost electric-feeling hands touched him. Tommy washed his back, hands running over Grayson's ass, and Grayson did his best to keep his legs from shaking. Once he'd rinsed as well, Tommy turned off the water, and Grayson grabbed towels for both of them.

Grayson dried Tommy's back for him and then got himself dry before taking care of the towels and scooting Tommy toward the bedroom. He brushed his teeth and straightened up before turning out the light.

Tommy was already in bed, lying on his back, staring up at the ceiling, the bedding down around his hips.

"You need to stop thinking so much."

"How can I not?" Tommy pulled his hands from behind his hand to rest them next to him on the bedding, but other than that, he didn't move.

"Because you don't have to do all of this alone. I know Xavier is being a jerk and he's pushing you, trying to get you upset and keep you off-kilter. It's how he gets what he wants from you. But you aren't alone. Petey and I are here, and as you can tell, Petey will stand up for you, and he'll fight Xavier with whatever he has. And I'll do the same."

"But you shouldn't have to," Tommy said, shifting slightly.

"Maybe that's true." Grayson walked around to the far side of the bed.

"I know it is."

God, sometimes Tommy could be such a stubborn mule.

"But I also think it's true that if things were reversed, you'd be the first one to help me." Grayson tugged up the covers and rolled over on his side. "You'd have called your aunt to get her help, and you'd be there for me. Hell, you'd be the first one to offer me money if I needed it, or just to come over to watch movies and play video games with Petey. Don't you know you're always there for me?"

Tommy shook his head. "Xavier told me more than once that I was distant and that my work was more important than him. So I used to stop what I was doing whenever he came over and we'd go out to wherever he wanted. I'd usually sit across from his friends while they all ignored me and talked about their shit. You remember the balloon game, *Flight of Fantasy*? I got that idea while I was out with Xavier because I was so bored and there was a party on the other side of the restaurant that had bunches of balloons tied to the seats around the table. The balloons weren't fastened well, and they started floating toward the ceiling."

"So Xavier was a jackass and expected you to be what he wanted instead of yourself. You have to be you," Grayson added as he tugged Tommy closer. "You can't be anyone else."

"But what if I'm not good enough?"

Grayson sighed, burying his face in Tommy's neck. "Then they don't deserve you. It's as simple as that. Xavier was the jerk, not you." He stroked Tommy's chest. "You're the one who's there to help."

Tommy got out of bed, standing. "Look at me. I'm a total nerd. The room is practically pitch-black and I'm so pale, I almost glow. I can't go out in the sun because I'll burn. And it's always this way. Just like I'm short, skinny as hell, and I'm never going to have an ass." He turned around. "See? There's nothing there." He turned back to face Grayson, who smiled, just taking in the view. "Are you listening to me?"

"Sort of. Mostly you sound like the adults on Charlie Brown. *Blah, blah, blah*. See, I like skinny guys, and as for your butt, well, that's also in the beholder and I like holding yours. What does it matter? I'm older than you, which means I'm going to get gray hair first, and probably arthritis and God knows what." Grayson rolled to the side of the bed and sat on the edge, drawing Tommy into his arms to stand between his legs. Then he rested his head on Tommy's belly. "You are the man you are, and believe it or not, that's good enough. You don't need to be someone else. Just be yourself and let us help you."

"But this really is my fight."

Grayson leaned back to look up at him. "Do you want to fight it alone? Or is this some misplaced honor thing? We all need help sometimes."

"I don't know what it is." Tommy wrapped his arms around Grayson's head, holding him. "But I don't want you and Petey tainted by him."

"Well, if we get rid of him for good and out of your life, then no one is going to be tainted by him. He can go on his merry way and find someone else to sponge off of." Grayson tugged Tommy close once again. "In a way I'm grateful to the guy. If he wasn't such a jerk and didn't get cold feet so bad his legs were frozen, then I wouldn't be here with you, and I never would have gotten the guts to say how I felt. We'll just deal with the jerkface and then we'll move on. And yes, I said 'we.' And the first thing we're going to do in the morning is let the resort know that Xavier has been back and let them take care of keeping him off the property. Then we'll call your aunt and sic her on him. Xavier isn't going to know what the hell hit him."

Tommy held him tighter. "I keep wondering what's going to happen if everything falls through. I can't lose my house. It's one of a kind—the gift I bought myself after my first hit. I mean, it's special and it has a soul. It does, and I won't lose it."

Grayson lifted his gaze. "Xavier doesn't want it—he's just a soulless bastard. All he wants is money, and he'll do whatever he has to in order to get it. And your aunt knows how to handle people like that." He guided Tommy back onto the bed. "We'll call her in the morning if we don't hear from her."

"Okay." Tommy lay back, and Grayson rested against him, his arms slinking around Tommy's waist.

"Good. Now it's time to sleep, because you know as well as I do that Petey is going to be up early and asking when he's going to be able to go on that boat ride you promised him. He's also counting the days until the sailboat excursion and everything else."

"He's sure taken with this place," Tommy commented, then yawned.

"Yes, he is. I also think he's taken with his uncle Tommy and the prospect that you could become more than his uncle." Grayson knew Petey was happy with his new relationship with Tommy, and Lord knew Grayson was happy with the way things were.

"There's a but in there. I can hear it, and I feel it too. This is paradise, and somehow we'll kick Xavier off it so we can be here in peace. But things will be different when we get home. I don't know what that's going to look like, and neither do you."

Grayson pulled him closer. "I can hope, though, and part of it, I hope, involves a bed as big as this one for just the two of us."

"Is that what you want?" Tommy asked.

Grayson kissed the back of Tommy's shoulder. "Sometimes what I want isn't as important as what you want." He sighed and tried to find the words, but they were on the tip of his tongue as soon as he opened his mouth. "You really don't get it, do you?"

"What is there to get?" Tommy tensed.

"That I see you. I already know what you look like naked. I've seen you and I got to feel you. Remember? I know that you have a huge heart and a creative soul that's demanding as hell, and that if you don't feed it, the creativity feels like it's going to explode. I know you get nervous and upset about things you can't control, so you have a tendency to organize everything to the point where you suck the fun out of it. And you're a workaholic, completely and totally. See, I know all that. You work so much sometimes, you get lost and forget to eat, and you once got so dehydrated, you had to go to the hospital."

Tommy gasped, and Grayson heard the tears in his voice. "Then why are you here if I'm so bad?"

"That's just it. You're a workaholic, and it'll be my job to make sure you eat and have something to drink. I'll also pat you on the shoulder to tell you to let it go and just have some fun. It'll be my job to encourage your creative side and still make sure you have time and the energy for a life outside of work. That will be my part of the relationship. I also know you're loyal and caring beyond belief. I have never met anyone with a bigger heart than you."

Tommy was quiet for a while. "You really feel that way?"

"Of course I do. Loving someone isn't for the money or the easy times, but the long haul. Not that I have a lot of experience with long-term relationships. The longest one I've had with anyone is with Petey, though that's very different. But just like the man I love, my relationship with my son is a lifetime commitment." Grayson kissed Tommy once again.

"But this is different."

"I think love is different with every person you love. I know you loved Xavier. Is what you felt for him the same as you feel for me?" In a way, Grayson was afraid of the answer. That question laid all his fears on the table, and that was always frightening.

"Of course not." Tommy rolled over. "You've been my best friend for years. I know that at first the thought of being a father scared you to death, but you got over it fast. You always persevered with whatever was thrown at you. It's one of the things I always loved about you. Nothing ever gets you down." Tommy stroked his cheek gently, shifting closer. "I see you too. I know you for the man you are. It's why I love you."

"Then how about we stop worrying about what might be and enjoy what we have?" Grayson suggested, and Tommy nestled close.

"I'll try." He sighed. "I guess I never really thought I could ever catch the interest of someone like you. It's hard to believe that a sex-on-a-stick-hot guy like you could be interested in a nerd like me." He smiled and kissed him hard. Grayson loved the way Tommy kissed, with fire and passion in each caress.

"Then I think it's time you adjusted your perspective. I know that's hard to do, but it's time you saw yourself as just as worthy as anyone else." Grayson smiled. "See, I love you because I see you and you see me. What more could we ask for?"

"Then we'll have to see," Tommy said, and Grayson didn't have the fight to argue with him. Not right now. Not that Tommy was wrong and Grayson hadn't wondered the same thing. He yawned and figured it was time to give up on all this thinking.

"How about we go to bed and think about it tomorrow?" Grayson closed his eyes, nestling his nose against Tommy's skin. He inhaled the rich scent and groaned softly. This was what he wanted, but how did he get Tommy to see that he did feel that Tommy was right for him? He knew his doubt and worry was because of Xavier, and maybe starting something with him wasn't a good idea. Maybe it was too soon and Tommy needed time. If that was the case, then Grayson would give him what he needed. But, damn, there were some times when patience sucked.

Chapter Seven

"**TOMMY,** I got your message about Xavier and the paperwork. I already put the process in motion for legal separation. Public announcement has been made that you are no longer responsible in any way for Xavier's actions and that he doesn't speak for you at all."

"Good. But what about the papers he has for the house? They were to have been destroyed." Tommy paced the bungalow, thankful that Grayson and Petey had gone to breakfast.

"Did you ever give him copies?"

"No." He stopped. "The only ones I had were mine, and they were in the house."

Aunt Ginny chuckled. "So he had to have stolen them. Good. If that ass contacts you again, inform him that, legally, he isn't allowed to profit from illegal activity.

He broke into your house to get those papers. The hard part is that we have to prove it. Where did you keep them?"

"In the file drawer in my office."

"I'll get the key from your father and take a look, but you don't have anything to worry about. I'll call the appropriate departments with the county and warn them that possibly stolen and fraudulent paperwork might be used to register the transaction. They won't accept it, and that should head him off. With the public notice to back it up, they'll listen." Up until now Aunt Ginny had been all business, but her voice softened as she asked, "How are you holding up there?"

"I'm doing well for the most part, except for Xavier." He told her about Petey pushing him into the water. "He looked like a drowned rat when he climbed out." Tommy laughed nervously.

"Xavier doesn't have a leg to stand on, so don't worry about him and whatever game he's playing. The guy is an ass, and I know how to handle men like him. Just relax and have a good time, and if your ex gets in the way again, give him another dunking. And whatever you do, don't worry about any of the legal stuff. I have everything well in hand. He isn't going to get half your house or a piece of anything else."

"I think what he wants more than anything is for me to drop the lawsuit about the wedding expenses," Tommy explained.

She sighed. "Of course he does, and he's going to pester you and try to get under your skin. I can file a restraining order here, but it isn't going to have any effect in Bonaire. Just stay with your friends and let them help provide a buffer. Don't listen to him, and if you can help it, stay away from him all together."

"Believe me, I don't want to have anything to do with him at all. I wish he'd go away, but I know he's going to hang around and try to see me and get under my skin any way he can."

"Do your best to have a good time, and kick the guy in the nuts if you have to." She chuckled. "I'm serious. Relax. I have things well in hand, and we'll cut off any avenues Xavier thinks he may have to get to you."

"Thanks." He felt better, was glad Aunt Ginny was on his side.

"I'll call you if anything changes. But just have a good time."

They disconnected, and Tommy took a few minutes to call his parents to let them know he was okay before going to join Grayson and Petey. He wasn't really hungry, but as soon as he sat down and smelled food, he ordered and ate better than he had in a while.

"What did she say?" Grayson asked, and Tommy gave him the basic rundown. "So are you going to file a restraining order?"

"I'm beginning to think that I may need one. He came all the way here to harass me, so it will be even easier for him to do it at home." The server brought his juice, and Tommy ate, trying his best to do what his aunt told him and forget about Xavier and his threats.

"Are we going boating?" Petey asked.

"Yes. Johan will bring the boat to our dock in an hour. I told him we'd be out the rest of the morning. So finish eating, and we'll get ready."

Petey was excited as anything, and Tommy did his best to show some energy and excitement for the day ahead. But he didn't feel it.

"What's going on upstairs?"

Tommy sighed. "I know I should be looking forward to having fun and all, but I'm going to be a downer. I want to work and escape. I know it's going to be just us and Xavier isn't going to bother me, but I have this—"

"You want to hide," Grayson said, and Tommy nodded. "And is that what you really want me to let you do? Stay in the bungalow behind your computer?" When Tommy didn't answer, Grayson sat quietly for a while. "I'm not going to sit here and make you come with us. Petey and I are going to go on the boat because I'm not going to disappoint him. What you do is up to you. There have been too many people trying to tell you what to do and how to act. Xavier tried to do it, and he still is. I won't."

Tommy set down his fork, swallowing his bite of eggs. "But—"

"No. I'm not going to tell you that you have to come. You can stay in the bungalow alone and work, or you can come with us and have some fun." The disappointment in Grayson's tone was clear, and Tommy hated that he was the source of it.

"You and Petey will have a better time without me," Tommy said, sure that was true.

Grayson stood, setting his napkin on the table. "Whatever you say. Come on, Petey. We're going to get ready." He and Petey left the dining room.

"Is Uncle Tommy coming?" Petey asked, turning to look back at him.

"I hope so," Grayson said, and they exited the room, leaving Tommy sitting alone.

Conversations swirled around him. Tommy drank his coffee, looking from table to table. Most were either couples or families, and they all seemed to be happy and excited. There was what appeared to be a newlywed couple on their honeymoon, just like he was supposed to be, only they were living their happiness while he sat alone. Just like always. He was usually the odd man out.

Tommy lowered his gaze and then covered his eyes. All he'd ever hoped for was someone to be his and his alone. Someone to care for him and be there for him whenever he needed it. Tommy squeezed his eyes closed as a wave of grief the size of a tsunami slammed into him. For the last week, he'd thought he'd been dealing with his loss, and maybe he had. But he couldn't have been. He was alone and…. Tears welled behind his hands, and he let them fall. This was supposed to be the happiest trip of his life, and here he was, alone in the dining room, crying. What was really pathetic was that people who cared for him were at the bungalow, getting ready to do something fun, and all he'd wanted to do was hide.

Tommy couldn't blame Grayson for leaving and losing patience with him. He was upset at himself. Sometimes things became overwhelming, and that was what was happening right now.

"Uncle Tommy?"

He lowered his hands to see Petey standing next to the table.

"Come on." Petey held out his hand, and Tommy wiped his wet palm on his napkin. He lifted his gaze, this time seeing Grayson standing in the doorway. "We're going to go boating."

Tommy nodded, finished his coffee, and stood. Petey tugged him toward the door and then out onto the sidewalk that ran the length of the resort to their bungalow.

"Daddy asked me to check on you. He said you might be mad at him, but that you'd never get mad at me. So I came to get you." Petey rushed him along. "We're going to miss the boat if we don't hurry."

"It's going to be fine, Petey," Grayson said softly from behind him. "We won't miss the boat." They reached door, and Tommy went inside, feeling blank. He wasn't sure what he was supposed to feel, but numb was probably as good as anything else. The red bag they'd been using for outings rested near the door.

"He was crying, Dad." Petey sounded like he was going to do the same.

"I know." Grayson took Tommy's other hand. "Why don't you watch out the door and let us know when the boat is coming."

Petey let go of his hand, and Grayson hugged Tommy. "It's okay. I shouldn't have left you alone." He rubbed Tommy's back. "I think I put too much on you."

"It's not your fault. I just find it hard to believe that someone would care as much as you do. I usually deal with things by hiding and letting my brain work through it. But maybe this is too big for that. I don't know. It feels like Xavier left me yesterday, and it hurts, Grayson. It really hurts." Tommy sniffed softly, wishing he had a tissue.

"What do you want to do?"

"I don't know. I'm not going to be much fun."

"And you do realize that going boating without you isn't going to be as much fun for Petey and me?" Grayson held him tighter. "Both of us would wonder about you, and then there would be something cool to see and I'd want to show it to you or see what your reaction would be…." Grayson smoothed away the tear tracks on Tommy's cheeks. "So don't shut yourself off—come with us."

Tommy nodded.

"Dad, Johan is here," Petey said, opening the patio door, sliding it back, but staying just inside. He called excitedly to Johan.

"I'm going to be okay," Tommy said, his throat a little sore.

"Then go wash your face and wipe your eyes if you want. I'll get things ready, and you can meet us at the boat." Grayson squeezed him one more time, then released him.

Tommy went right to his room—their room—and into the bathroom. He ran some water, splashing it on his face. Then he dried himself and grabbed a tissue to blow his nose, looking at himself in the mirror. It was time for him to put on his big-boy panties and get over himself. What happened had happened, and there was nothing he could do about it, except concentrate on the two people out there, waiting for him. They cared, and they'd come back for him even when he'd tried to pull away.

He left the bathroom and joined the others out on the dock. Grayson locked up behind them and took his hand to lead him out to the boat.

"Welcome!" Johan said. "Are you ready for some fun? I thought we'd head around to the other side of Bonaire. It's part of the island that visitors don't see very often. It's pretty and can be rough, but today the water is calm."

They got on the boat, seated themselves under the sun shade, with Tommy applying sunscreen anyway, and Johan pulled away from the dock, heading out away from the resort and toward open water.

Tommy breathed deeply as water flowed by them, and peace settled into him once again. Petey and Grayson remained quiet so that only the sound of the wind and the engine filled the air. Tommy wished they had a sail so the engine wasn't necessary, but he tuned it out, listening to the wind. After a few minutes, he pulled off his shirt, letting the air get to his skin, and the weight on his shoulders lessened. It became easier to breathe, and his entire body was lighter. His lips curled upward. Petey and Grayson sat next to him, and the overall mood on the boat lightened as time went on.

"This area of the island… all the beaches are protected," Johan explained. "You can dive and snorkel if you want, but you mustn't touch or take anything."

"Are there any good swimming beaches?" Petey asked.

"No. This isn't that kind of island. Our beaches are coral ones, and you have to be careful. Before the regulations, some of the resorts brought in sand to try to build beaches, but the sea washed it away. That's why all the resorts offer snorkeling and diving. It's what we do best here. If you want great beaches, you go to Aruba. They have them. We have the diving." Johan smiled.

"I liked when we went," Petey said. "It was really special." He turned to Grayson. "I think I want to study reefs and fish when I get older. If I do, can I come here to live?" His eyes were huge and the smile on his face as bright as the tropical sun.

"Why don't we see about getting you through fourth grade first?" Grayson smiled. "But yes, you can do whatever you want when you grow up. I'll support and help you any way I can. If you want to study reefs and things, then you have to do really well in school. Have you given any thought to what you want to write in your report?"

Petey groaned.

"When we get back to the bungalow, I'll help you. But you have to think of the topic and what you want to say." Tommy caught Petey's eye, and he nodded. Clearly some of the wind had gone out of Petey's sails. "You just need to think about it."

"Maybe you could do something on the different kinds of sea life we have here. I'm sure you got great pictures. So you could talk about each of them," Johan offered.

"Yeah." Petey went on to list all of the different things he'd seen, his excitement returning just like that. Grayson put an arm around Petey's shoulders and the other around Tommy's.

"Now this is fun," Tommy whispered as he leaned back and let go for a while, spending time with the people he loved, the wind, and the water. The rest of the world didn't matter for a few hours.

"In a little while, we'll be coming up on the salt flats. That's where we harvest salt from the sea. We let the water in, dye it so it's dark, then let the sun burn off the water and harvest the salt left behind."

"Cool," Petey said, standing so he could look over the side. "I really like it here, Dad."

"So do I," Grayson said, turning to Tommy, his gaze staying on him, heating. Grayson tugged him closer, and they sat together quietly while Petey went to stand near Johan. "Feeling better?"

"I guess so." Tommy smiled. "Aunt Ginny has things well in hand, and she'll head off anything Xavier can try to pull from a legal perspective, but I keep wondering what he's going to try next. He's here on the island, and he's not going to sit by while what he wants goes flying out the window." Tommy shifted a little closer to Grayson. "I keep wondering what his deal is. He's the one who backed away and canceled the wedding. What did he expect was going to happen? That I'd be so grateful or ripped to shreds that I'd give him whatever he wanted just to make him go away once and for all? If he'd have gone through with the wedding, he could have had access to just about anything."

"Yes and no. Just because you were married didn't mean you had to add him to your credit cards or bank accounts. And while most assets become joint, he was going to have to stay with you for a period of time. If you split up right away, any court would be likely to simply return your assets to you because you had them before you were married. A lot of states have a type of gold-digger clause in the laws."

"How do you know so much?"

"I used to talk to your aunt at parties, and let me tell you, she's a barrel of laughs, especially once you get a few drinks in her. She can tell some of the best legal stories. Like dumb criminal tricks... except they're stupid lawsuit tricks. Your aunt knows what she's doing."

"Yeah, she does. But what I really want to know is, how do I get Xavier to go home and leave me alone? I don't want to see him again... ever." Tommy groaned. "Do you know that I keep watching for him, everywhere? I checked out all the tables at breakfast just to make sure he wasn't there. The resort said that he isn't staying here and asked if I'd notify them if he comes on the property again so they could escort him away. But I still looked. It's like I can't have fun because I'm scared he'll show up and take it away." Tommy's hand shook.

"You're giving him way too much power." Grayson's tone was gentle, but with authority behind it. "You wanted someone in your life, and you thought you had Xavier so you let him decide things for you. Am I right?"

Tommy had to agree that was pretty close to the truth. He'd told Grayson about all that, and it was a fair assessment.

"Things like that don't just stop because something happens—it becomes ingrained."

Grayson patted his thigh lightly, and Tommy was grateful that Grayson didn't take his logic further. It wasn't a huge stretch of the imagination to see that, over time, things between him and Xavier would have degraded into something ugly and hurtful. They would have come to hate each other, and it was likely Xavier would have tried to control him. Tommy could see now that Xavier had already started down that road, and Tommy had just gone along with him because he'd been so desperate to have someone in his life and not be alone. He shivered and closed his eyes. Maybe he really had needed this trip so he could clear his head, be able to see things clearly, and move on.

"You have to be the one to stop it."

"How do I do that?" Tommy asked.

Grayson smiled. "You already are. You're thinking about it and you're aware of the games he's playing. He's a manipulative son of a bitch. What you need to do is decide that you aren't going to take it anymore and then figure out how you want to deliver the message." His smile grew wider and more devilish. "Just promise me you'll let me be there when you do."

Tommy stiffened. "Because you don't think I can handle it?"

"Hell no. Because I want to see the bastard's face when you do. He isn't going to know what hit him." Grayson laughed outright.

"Okay." Tommy smiled as well, really feeling it this time. With a deep breath, he let go of some of the pile of emotional manure Xavier had heaped on him and turned to look out to sea. "The water seems to go on forever."

"But it doesn't." Grayson pointed. "Just over the horizon, that direction, is South America, everything between Venezuela and Argentina. But we can't see it, at least not from here."

"No, we can't," Tommy agreed. Just like he hadn't seen the love he already had in his life because he was concentrating on things with Xavier. Tommy turned, and there was the island, the bastion of land and solidity in a sea of uncertainty. God, his mind went to some pretty weird crap when he let it. The truth was, he had what he'd always wanted, if Grayson wanted the same things he did. He thought and hoped so. But was he ready for it?

"You know, it's okay not to know what you want, or to want something and not know if it's the right thing. We all feel that way sometimes." Grayson patted his leg once again as Johan brought them in close.

Tommy sniffed and turned to Grayson, burying his face in his shoulder. Tommy wasn't used to not knowing his own mind and what he wanted. Being confused and scared really sucked. Other men got nasty and short when that happened; Tommy internalized it. He was determined not to cry, even if the fucking tears were close. He'd been trying to figure shit out for days, and maybe he was expecting too damned much of himself.

"I told you I wasn't going to be good company," Tommy said softly.

"You're just fine." Grayson lightly stroked his hair, and Tommy leaned even more against Grayson.

"How can you be so understanding about all this?"

Grayson scoffed in that way he had that sounded sort of like a duck. "You think you're the first person to have a broken heart? I have—I know how it feels and how it rips you up sometimes. It was hard as hell getting over Jeffrey. I lost a good friend, as well as someone I loved. You remember how hard a time I had. Thank God I had Petey to help keep me grounded and my head on straight… and you. Remember?"

Tommy nodded, lifting his head away from Grayson. "You were a mess for quite a while."

"And now I'm returning the favor." Grayson cupped his chin and kissed him gently. "You don't need to be ashamed."

"Dad, look! The dolphins are back." Petey pointed, and they all looked as the dolphins swam along with them. Petey nearly fell over the side, he was leaning so far to see them, and Tommy grabbed him by the belt.

"Dude, you need to be careful. You don't want to go swimming right now. Maybe later." They shared a smile, and Tommy stayed with Petey, trying to see things through his eyes. And as soon as he did, most of the worries and cares melted, and Tommy let some happiness wash over him. How could he not with a pair of dolphins jumping next to them, Petey laughing joyfully, and Grayson standing beside him, a hand on his back just to maintain contact?

Tommy grabbed his phone to snap a few pictures so Petey could use them as part of his report. "How much farther are we going?" he asked Johan.

"The island goes for miles more." Johan pointed. "I thought we'd see that outcropping there and then head back." He returned to watching what he was doing, and Tommy rejoined Petey, scanning the water around them.

"A turtle," Grayson called, pointing to where a large head skimmed along the water. Johan slowed and got close to where he was taking a breath. The shell was enormous, and Tommy got the best picture he could, snapping multiples in the hope that one would be suitable. Then the turtle was gone, and Johan sped up once again.

After a little while, Grayson broke out the snacks, and they all sat under the canopy, eating trail mix, drinking some soda, and, damn, Tommy was happy. Just like that, things had slipped into place. Grayson was right—he had been giving Xavier way too much power over him, and now he truly did need to figure out what he was going to do about it. The answers weren't coming, but Tommy would figure it out.

"I love the dolphins," Petey said as they picked up speed, their friends keeping up, jumping and having fun. Tommy wished he could let Petey jump into the water and swim with them. He'd be thrilled, and most of all, Tommy wanted to make Petey and Grayson happy. Maybe that was the magic in all this: doing something for someone else. Tommy doubted he had ever truly made Xavier happy or heard him laugh or saw him smile the way Grayson was.

"Me too." Tommy rubbed Petey's head. "This is the best."

They rode for another hour, and then Johan turned them back toward the resort. Unlike on their way out, they didn't meander and took an almost direct path. That didn't lessen the view of Grayson lounging back or the excitement that built of what was to come.

"Can we stay out longer?" Tommy asked.

Johan paused. "I have another appointment and a shift at the bar, and…."

Tommy nodded. "I understand. It's perfectly fine." He closed his eyes, deeply inhaling the salty air. There was something about it that sent a measure of peace into his soul, and dammit, he liked it and wanted it to continue. He drank his soda, watching as they drew closer and closer to the resort, their dock coming into view.

It was empty. No figure standing at the end waiting for them like the specter of death for his happiness and peace of mind. "Let's go to the pool," Tommy offered. "We can all go swimming for a while, and your dad and I can sit in the bar and keep Johan company, maybe have some lunch. Is that okay?" He knew it would be. Petey was always ready for a swim.

Grayson squeezed his hand once again as Johan pulled up to the dock. They got off and waved. Johan waved back before reversing the boat and speeding off.

Grayson got Petey ready for the pool, slathering him with an additional layer of sunscreen. The sun was brutal, and Grayson was already telling Petey that he couldn't be in the water too long. Tommy changed into his bathing suit and put on a sun shirt. Grayson did the same, only his pulled tight over his chest and at his arms. He wished he and Grayson could be alone for a while, but that wasn't possible right now.

"Get what you want to take with you," Grayson reminded Petey, and Petey hurried to his bedroom. As soon as the door closed, Grayson leaned close, his breath ghosting over Tommy's ear. "Don't worry. I have plans for us tonight. Petey is going to be very tired." He pulled Tommy into a kiss that grew heated within seconds. Tommy had never wanted anyone the way he did Grayson. Each touch sent ripples of fire racing through him.

Tommy knew what lust felt like. He'd experienced that plenty of times. In college, he used to watch the football players and go to the games just to see them in those tight shorts. They had been in his late-night fantasies for a very long time. Grayson was hot, sexy, and already almost indecent in his shorts, but Grayson made Tommy want more than sex. He wanted it all— the forever, the life, the family. But Tommy had long ago learned that he rarely got everything he wanted.

THE water felt good, but he still got out of the pool after a few minutes. He turned as he felt Grayson's intense gaze on him. Tommy let Grayson watch, a blush rising in his cheeks. Then he got out of the sun, wrapping himself in a towel and heading for a lounge chair in the shade. Tommy got comfortable, watching Grayson and Petey.

"Is this seat taken?"

Tommy knew that voice instantly. "What do want, Xavier? Can't you just leave me alone?" He didn't even look up at him. He was so proud that he kept his eyes down and did his best to not let Xavier get a rise out of him.

"We need to talk." The chair next to him squeaked on the concrete as Xavier sat down.

Tommy turned toward him. "Do we really? I don't think we have anything to talk about other than when you're going to pack up and go home."

"Have you given any thought to what we talked about before?" Xavier never raised his voice, but the threat was there nonetheless.

"Yes, I have. My lawyer has taken care of that. The papers were stolen, and the theft has been reported to the county. Your paperwork could never be filed. What you have is worthless, and trying to blackmail me with it in order to get something from me is low. Even for you."

Xavier sputtered, and Tommy smiled at his frustration. Xavier was used to getting what he wanted with his looks and his charm. But Tommy was way past all that now. Grayson was right—he had been giving Xavier way too much power over him, and that was going to stop.

"I couldn't go through with it. Doesn't that mean anything to you?"

"What? That you said you loved me and that you'd marry me and then left me at the altar? That you humiliated me and made me feel like I was two inches tall? I'm supposed to reward you for that?" Tommy stood as Grayson and Petey rushed over. "It's okay," he told both of them, his chest heaving with anger and pain. "Xavier and I are going to the bungalow to talk. Give me ten minutes and then send in the cavalry." He turned and left the pool area, heading to the bungalow without looking back to see if he was followed. He knew Xavier would be behind him. Tommy opened the door and went inside, then closed the door behind Xavier.

"Tommy, I did care. You have to know that." Xavier sounded sincere, but Tommy wasn't falling for that again.

He shook his head. "What you did was completely unfeeling. I know you were only interested in me for the money and that you backed away before that could get to be an issue. I am grateful for that. But what I don't understand is why you don't leave me alone and have your lawyer answer the lawsuit? You could have taken care of business at home. You didn't have to come here."

"Yes, I did. You were suing me and, well… I made a mistake. I shouldn't have walked away like that and…."

Tommy sighed, taking the chance to consider his words. "You pulled all this crap because you wanted me back? Come on. That's so damn cliché. You only wanted the money."

"No, I didn't. I really did care for you, just not the way I should have when we were going to get married. I ended up getting drunk before the wedding, spending a lot of time with my friends, and they… well, they started saying how cool it was going to be once you and I were married. I'd have access to your money and everything was going to be perfect. There'd be parties, and you and I would be going places and having all this fun… but we'd never do that because you work all the time. That started me drinking more because I thought we weren't going to be happy, and then… shit, I don't know. I got scared and backed away. You were better off without me, and…."

Tommy crossed his arms over his chest. "Why did you try to charge that watch?"

"Gary did. He figured that if I was going to leave, I should see if I could get something out of it. So he tried charging it, but the transaction was declined." Xavier sighed. "I'm glad, because you didn't deserve to be stolen from." He looked around and sat down in one of the chairs. "I messed everything up, I know that. I do. I should have stayed away. But I knew if I could talk to you, I could make you see reason. I don't have anything, and I can't afford a lawyer and stuff. All I have is my job and my car."

Tommy leaned against the wall. "You know, I would have given you anything you liked. I bought you a car as a wedding present, and I would have tried to take care of you." He blinked hard. "I loved you, but I see you didn't love me." He looked downward. "When I met you, I wondered how a guy like you could be interested in someone like me, and I didn't understand it. But I do now. I'm a good person and I have feelings and I deserve to be happy."

The bungalow door opened, Grayson and Petey hurrying inside. "You said ten minutes, and I kept track," Petey said, waving Grayson's phone.

"Xavier is leaving, and we won't be seeing him again." Tommy stood upright. "There is nothing he can get from me. As for the paperwork, he's going to get it and return what he stole or he will face charges of attempted robbery and extortion. I'll see to that." He wasn't going to let Xavier off the hook.

"Tommy, you can't be serious," Xavier said, shaking a little.

"You're damn right I am." Tommy turned to Xavier with fire in his eyes. "We are done. I want nothing more to do with you, which is exactly what happened after you left me. I'll talk to my aunt about the lawsuit." He leaned forward. "But not for your sake—for theirs." He turned to Grayson and Petey. "I want them... us... to be able to figure things out without dealing with you any longer." Tommy smiled. "See, you leaving did me a favor, so I'm doing that in return." He held out his hand, and Grayson took it.

"I always knew there was something going on between you," Xavier crowed. "You said you were just friends and all that, but I knew there was something more."

"There wasn't," Grayson said. "Not until you left and he asked us to come to keep him company. Things have developed between us, and we're seeing how they go."

Xavier stood, turning to Tommy. "He only wants you for your money. That's—"

"All you wanted, so it's all you think others want. Your projections onto others reveal who you really are." Tommy raised his eyebrows. "I'll give you credit for doing the right thing in the end, even if it was a shitty way of going about it. Now I want you to leave—this bungalow, the resort, and this island. My lawyer will be in touch regarding anything else between us." He stepped forward. "Understand me clearly: we are done."

Xavier humphed, staying where he was. Tommy pointed, and eventually his ex left the bungalow. Petey closed the door and locked it.

"Goodbye, scumbag." Petey leaned against the door, grinning. "He's really gone, isn't he?"

Tommy cleared his throat as he blinked, realizing what he'd just done. "I think so." Damn, he felt a million pounds lighter. His husband-to-be had left him, and now he had what he really wanted. "I feel like singing, but I won't because it'll hurt your ears." He grinned and did a little dance to the music in his head, shaking his hips and moving through the living area. Then Grayson was there, holding him, moving with him, and Tommy closed his eyes, going with it.

"You can dance too," Grayson told Petey, extending his hand. Soon all three of them were dancing together, having a good time. Tommy's spirit felt lighter than it had in so very long. He held on to Grayson, because without him he would never have gotten over Xavier or figured out that what he already had was so much better than anything he had been looking for.

"I love you," Tommy whispered to Grayson, then looked down at Petey. "I love you too." Right now, he didn't need to hear the words in return; he knew they were true from the smile on Petey's face and the heat in Grayson's eyes. That told him everything he ever needed to know.

AFTER spending part of the afternoon in the pool and then having dinner, Petey was worn out. They watched *The Legend of Tarzan*, which was a great choice. Petey loved the story and the scenery, and with Tarzan muscularly shirtless for a lot of the movie, that was nothing to sneeze at either. Though Tarzan had nothing on Grayson, in Tommy's opinion anyway. Petey went right to bed almost as soon as it ended. Just like they had other nights, the stars and moon seemed to tug Tommy outside. He sat on the dock, feeling as well as hearing Grayson walking up behind him. Unlike those first nights, the tentativeness was gone. He sat down, tugged Tommy's T-shirt over his head, and then pressed to him, the tropical sea air surrounding them.

"You did so amazingly well today," Grayson whispered. "I loved how you stood up for yourself and handled Xavier."

Tommy nodded. "Me too."

"Do you have any regrets?" Grayson slowly slid his magic hands up and down Tommy's chest, languidly stoking the fire that rapidly built inside him.

Tommy chuckled. "You mean, other than asking him to marry me in the first place and putting myself through all this crap? Nope." He knew Grayson was smiling behind him. Tommy could see it in his mind's eye. "About telling him to take a hike and leave me alone? No. You were right. I needed to tell him that I wasn't going to let him influence my life. He'd already done enough of that when we were together, and it isn't going to happen any longer." Tommy arched his back so he could glimpse Grayson's eyes. "I really don't think we're going to be seeing any more of him, and I wouldn't be surprised if he's already booking his trip home." He leaned back farther so he could kiss Grayson.

"So you're happy."

"Yes. I'm happy. You and Petey make me happy. You always have." He shifted on the dock. "I guess I'm starting to wonder just how dumb I am that I wasn't able to see what was in front of me all along. You've been in my life for years, and you've always been there for me."

"So have you, and while I liked you and carried this thing with me, I never did anything about it." Grayson sighed, and Tommy turned back around, looking out at the myriad of stars twinkling and dancing off the nearly still water. "I wish I had said something."

"I don't. Things happen for a reason, and we both had to be ready for whatever we have between us in order for it to work. Maybe I needed to kiss a few frogs and date a troll before I could see what was right in front of me. Xavier was my troll, and Jeffrey was yours." Tommy thought for a second. "If we get things right the first time around, then we wonder if what we have is really good enough. Maybe kissing the frogs is necessary before we know when we've found our prince." And Tommy was sure he'd found his; he knew it in his heart. "What do we do when we get home?"

"We'll figure it out. You and I don't have to have all the answers now. We can see how things go, date, spend more time together, and then decide what we want to do. Just because we've been friends doesn't mean we have to do anything differently than we would if we were just getting to know each other."

"But I already know you, and...." Tommy grew quiet as the wisdom of what Grayson was saying sank in.

"I know you too. But getting involved with me also means being part of Petey's life, and that's a big commitment. You need to know what that's like, and he needs a chance to get used to having you around. So we'll do some things as a family and some things just the two of us." Grayson kissed his shoulder, then sucked a trail to his neck. "Just relax and go with it. Everything doesn't need to be planned out, and you don't need to have all the answers up front."

"You know that's hard for me."

"But relationships don't work like that." He squeezed a little tighter. "How about we go inside? I think it's bedtime."

Tommy shivered, but cold was the last thing on his mind. He didn't want to move and leaned back once again. Grayson cradled him, holding him tightly, and kissed him, stopping his breathing. He could have stayed like this forever, except his pants were cutting off the circulation to his cock and he desperately needed to get out of them. Thankfully Grayson seemed to sense it. He stood, then helped Tommy to his feet. Taking Tommy's hand, Grayson led him inside and closed the sliding door.

"Go on to the bedroom and get ready for me. I need to check on Petey." Grayson went to the other room, and Tommy entered his, slipped out of his clothes, and settled on the mattress. Grayson came in a minute later, closing the door after him, and just stood there. "Wow."

Tommy smiled. "Sometimes I wonder if you need to have your eyes checked, and then I think… no… don't you dare. I want you to see me as—"

"Sweetheart, I see you without any trouble." Grayson kicked off his shoes and dropped his shorts, stepping out of them. The last of his clothes hit the floor, and Grayson joined him on the bed. "I've always seen you for who you are. What I want to do is help you see yourself the way I see you." Grayson climbed over Tommy, pushing him onto his back.

"And I see you too."

"I never had any doubts about that. Not since the first day we met, when I was with Jeffrey, and now." Grayson leaned forward, capturing Tommy's lips, and what he wanted to say died as his brain short-circuited. This wasn't the time for a conversation, at least not the kind that was spoken. Tommy intended to let his body do the talking, and as Grayson pressed to him, he knew it was going to be one hell of a conversation.

Tommy's mind blew out after a few minutes, becoming only sensation and affection. Grayson made him forget everything, including his damn name, with just a few kisses. After that, he held on as Grayson loved on him with his lips, taking him deep, bringing Tommy to the brink within seconds and then backing away. Time and time again, he brought Tommy close, and each time, just before he might tumble into the abyss of bliss and joy, Grayson pulled him back. Delicious frustration built to unbelievable levels. Tommy growled under his breath, swearing softly about all the things he intended to do to Grayson, including something about ripping his gorgeous face off if he didn't let him come.

"Not yet," Grayson said with such gentleness and care before flipping Tommy over, tugging his hips upward, and burying his face between Tommy's cheeks, sending a whole new round of mind-exploding delight washing over him.

"When? After I'm dead?" he mumbled half into the pillow, gripping it for dear life.

Grayson probed him, hot and wet, as Tommy quivered from head to toe. "If this kills you, I guarantee you'll die ecstatic."

Tommy reached up and gripped the headboard, Grayson's hands kneading his cheeks, tongue licking and probing him. Tommy ground his hips into the sheet for just enough sensation to....

Grayson tugged his hips upward, opening Tommy more to his ministrations of delight, which threatened to overwhelm him completely. He held on to his very identity and essence for fear they'd be lost in Grayson and the way he made him feel. Tommy thought he'd known happiness before, but today he knew bliss—hot, sweaty, wet, mind-melting bliss that seemed to go on forever.

Until Grayson stopped.

"What happened?" he asked, not realizing he'd said it out loud until his confusion was greeted by soft chuckles.

"Roll over, gorgeous," Grayson whispered, and Tommy complied without thought. He hadn't heard the rip of the condom packet or even the snick of the bottle of lube, but when he settled on his back, Grayson gently gripped his ankles, parted them, and slid between his legs.

"Oh God," Tommy whimpered, and Grayson filled him with sweet, agonizing slowness until Tommy's eyes crossed. Grayson gave him all he needed, and the last bit of himself that he'd been holding on to flew out of his grasp. He belonged to Grayson. No, he gave himself to Grayson. What surprised Tommy was that he expected to feel empty, but Grayson gave right back, and somehow Tommy ended up with more than he'd ever had before. He was loved—about that he had no doubt.

"Yes, honey. You can say that again." Grayson leaned over him, bringing their lips together, and sent Tommy over the moon. He had no idea how or why, but he held Grayson, and within seconds a wave of heat slammed into him and the release he'd been denied broke over him like one of the waves on the sea outside their window.

It was all he'd ever wanted and more, and Tommy had it. Now he just needed to hold on to it.

Chapter Eight

GRAYSON woke with Tommy pressed to him, half glued to him. It was still completely dark, but between the sweat and the residue from the lovemaking from heaven, they were kind of stuck.

"Don't make me move," Tommy groaned from his embrace. "If we do, then I'll wake up and all this will be a dream."

"*Daddy*!" Petey cried, and Grayson jumped.

"Go," Tommy said instantly, and Grayson climbed off the bed, yanked on his shorts, and hurried out of the room. It both amazed and terrified him just how much Tommy seemed to understand what he needed to do.

He arrived in Petey's room and sat on the edge of his bed as Petey tossed, nearly rolling out, the sheet wrapping him like a burrito. Petey struggled as Grayson got him untangled. "What happened?"

"Daddy," Petey said, blinking awake. "I thought you were gone." He rubbed his eyes. "I thought Uncle Tommy had taken you and I was all alone." He lowered his gaze.

"Honey. My boy." Grayson hugged him tight. "I love you, and I'd never leave you behind. Not for anything. Uncle Tommy loves you too, and he'd never leave you behind either."

"But you're going to be boyfriends and you'll do stuff you don't want me to see and you'll go places and leave me." Petey clutched him. "What if you don't want me anymore and then I have to go live with Mommy in a grass hut or something, like those people in that Tarzan movie?"

Grayson squeezed him, putting a hand on his head. "You are the most important person to me, and you always will be. Uncle Tommy knows that. Neither of us is going to let you go to Africa unless we all go together." God, sometimes he never considered the effect a movie was going to have. "I promise you that." He lifted Petey's chin. "You're my son and I love you so much." He hugged Petey, then straightened out the covers on his bed and got him settled once more.

Petey lay back down. "Are you sure?"

Grayson rubbed his back, soothing him gently. "Yes. I'm as sure of that as I am of anything else in the world." He waited until Petey dozed off before leaving the room. He returned to Tommy's bedroom, expecting to find him asleep again, but Tommy came out of the bathroom, where a low light burned. He took Grayson by the hand, led him inside, and started the shower. Then he slipped off Grayson's shorts before guiding him under the spray.

The hot water was soothing, both for his body and his jangled nerves. He hated to admit it, but the conversation with Petey had made him nervous. He'd been going full steam ahead with things with Tommy and hadn't stopped for very long to consider how it might be making Petey feel.

"I heard part of what Petey said," Tommy whispered above the sound of the shower. "You know I love Petey and don't want to hurt him."

"Then you heard what I said. He's had me all to himself for six years, other than when I was with Jeffrey, and things were different then. He was younger and he wasn't as able to express himself. I also think he had a nightmare and a bunch of weirdness from the movie he watched, so things got a little mixed up in his head." Grayson leaned back as Tommy soaped his hands, then stroked his chest and down to his legs.

"So…." Tommy seemed nervous; Grayson read it in his eyes.

"Petey loves you. He's just a little nervous, probably rightly so, that our lives are going to change. Jeffrey left a bad taste for both of us. Petey needs some time to get used to things." Grayson groaned as Tommy massaged his shoulders. "I mean, we've talked about how rapidly our relationship has progressed between us, and it's faster for him. He's a kid, and it's out of his control." Grayson sighed. "I suppose if he just went along and never said anything, I'd be worried." He felt like a bad parent. He should have anticipated this sort of situation.

"I understand if you need some time with him." Tommy stepped back, tugging Grayson gently under the water to rinse. "If you feel you need to go back to the other room and slow down, I will understand. He's your son, and I don't want to cause trouble for you."

Grayson wasn't sure what the right thing to do was. He knew what he wanted, and it was to stay where he was. But maybe he should do what Petey might need and go back to the other room. Slow things down and give Petey a chance to adjust. "I'm not going to get any answers tonight."

"I know. Let's finish cleaning up, and you can figure things out in the morning." Tommy turned him around, soaped up his back, and then Grayson returned the favor, growing excited by Tommy's skin under his hands. He'd never get enough of this. Tommy was like a drug for him—the more he got, the more he craved and needed. This whole thing was almost too much and yet not enough, all at the same time.

Once Tommy was clean, he turned off the water and grabbed towels. They dried off and stepped out into the bedroom, letting their bodies cool before climbing into bed. Tommy held his hand, falling to sleep, while Grayson remained awake, his mind unable to shut off.

"PETEY," Grayson called, sitting out on the dock, watching the water as he drank his cup of coffee the following morning.

"Dad?" Petey answered, hurrying out.

"I need to talk to you." Grayson had been awake most of the night and figured the best course of action was to talk with Petey and find out what he really felt.

Petey came up beside him, barely able to stand still. "What did I do?"

Grayson gestured for him to sit and put an arm around Petey's shoulders when he complied. "Nothing bad." He turned to look him in the eye. "You know that your Uncle Tommy and I… well, we're trying to figure stuff out." Grayson cleared his throat. "I'm hoping that Uncle Tommy and I will become serious and that things change between us. But I need to know if that's okay with you."

Petey scrunched his eyebrows. "You're asking me if it's okay if you date him?"

"Yes. We're a family, you and me. And I don't want you to feel hurt or slighted. So I thought I should ask you what you felt. You had a nightmare last night and called for me. You were scared, and I think that might have been because of what's been happening."

Petey nodded. "So you're asking my permission?"

"Yes."

Petey bit his lower lip. "And what will you do if I said that I didn't want you to?" He looked away, out over the water. "I don't want things to be like with Jeffrey. He was a jerk and was pretty stinky. He didn't like me and only wanted you." He turned back to Grayson.

"Do you think Tommy is that way?"

Petey shrugged, and Grayson narrowed his gaze. "No. But what if he gets that way?"

"Tommy has known you since you came to live with me. Do you really think he's going to decide he doesn't like you?" Grayson shook his head. "I don't think so. Things between you and Uncle Tommy aren't going to change except that instead of an uncle, he'll be like a second dad… if that's what you want."

"Is he going to live in our house?" Petey asked.

"I don't know. He and I haven't talked about stuff like that. I do know we aren't going to make any changes to our lives quickly. We'll figure things out. But I want you to know that what affects both of us, you and I will talk about." He tugged Petey into a hug. "I want you to be happy."

"You need to be happy too, Dad," Petey told him, and just like that, another piece of the child, his child, fell away to reveal the initial outlines of the man Petey was going to become.

"I will be happy. I am happy. How can I not be with you for a son?" Grayson held him tighter, trying to imagine what he had done to have gotten so lucky. "I love you so much." He tried to keep the tears out of his voice, but it was difficult beyond belief. "You're not my baby anymore."

"Dad...," Petey groaned.

"When you first came to live with me, you were a toddler. You liked it when I lifted you over my head and flew you around the room. You used to give the same answer to every question. *No.* It didn't matter what it was, you never answered yes. If I asked if you wanted some ice cream, you'd grin, but you never said yes. Then you got older and started talking all the time, went to school, made friends, and now you're becoming a young man." It was hard seeing him growing up. "Yes, you get a say in the way we live our lives."

"Okay. I like Uncle Tommy."

Grayson hugged Petey once again. "Good. So do I."

"When are we going home?"

"The day after tomorrow is our last day here. We're going snorkeling again this afternoon." Grayson released Petey, and he hurried inside. Soon Grayson heard the video game start up. Sometimes it was good to see the kid in him again.

"Is everything okay?" Tommy asked, coming out a little while later.

"Yes. Petey seems okay with things, and he's looking forward to snorkeling again. Maybe tomorrow we can take him boating one last time before we leave." Grayson was going to be sorry to see this trip end. What he'd thought would be a trip to help Tommy get over his pain had turned into something completely different, and going back to the real world didn't hold much appeal. "I think some quiet time is in order for a few hours."

"Good." Tommy leaned close to kiss him and went back inside. Grayson knew Tommy would be in his room with the door closed, and sure enough, when he checked on him an hour later, he was bent over his computer, lost in a world of his own making.

Grayson ordered lunch to be brought to the bungalow for them and took some in to Tommy, then left him alone once again. He and Petey ate together, lazing around until it was time for them to get ready to go. Petey went to change, and Grayson interrupted Tommy.

"We're getting ready for the snorkel." Grayson passed Tommy his suit and the water shirt. "Put these on, and we'll get you sunblocked up."

Tommy saved his work and closed the computer. Then he sat back, his eyes a little glazed. Grayson knew he was bringing his brain out of his own world and into the real one. "Okay. Is this going to be different from the last one?"

"I don't know. We're supposed to be snorkeling in a new location, so we'll have to see. We need to meet at the main resort dock in ten minutes, so change and we'll get you ready to go." Grayson used the time that Tommy was dressing to pack their bag and put on sunblock, then gooped up Tommy. He also checked on Petey, and they were all well coated before leaving the bungalow for their excursion.

Grayson locked the door and strode between Tommy and Petey to the dock, where a beautiful catamaran waited for them. The hull was blue and white, shining in the sun.

The mate helped them board, and they took seats under the sun shade.

"Welcome aboard," a young woman with a slight Dutch accent said. "I'm Kayla, and we're going to have a great time this afternoon. Our captain is Ronnie, and we also have Julio as crew. Clark will be here for all your snack and drink needs. Everything is complimentary, and once the snorkeling is done, the bar will be open to serve alcohol. Until then, we have soda and punch, so don't be shy." She smiled as Tommy, Petey, Grayson, and the seven or eight other guests got settled. Then they pulled away from the dock and out onto the water.

THE snorkeling was great, and the day had been even more wonderful. The sun was bright, penetrating deep under the water, lighting the coral and fish, creating spectacular color. It took Grayson's breath away, and that was saying a lot, breathing through a snorkel.

"We need to get on board," Grayson said, helping them toward the back of the boat. "Go on," he told Petey and got him to climb the steps. Grayson took his flippers off and handed them to a deckhand, then treaded water as Tommy climbed the ladder behind Petey.

"What's that?" Petey asked, pointing, as Grayson reached for the ladder. "It's getting closer."

"Grayson, get up now. That's a jellyfish." Tommy reached the top of the ladder quickly, but not fast enough.

Burning pain shot up and around Grayson's leg. He jumped up the ladder and flopped onto the deck, looking down at his leg. "What the hell?" Grayson gritted as the burning intensified. "Holy...." He hissed as someone poured salt water over his leg, multiple times. Kayla ran a soft cloth over his lower leg and then poured more water over it.

"We have to get what the tentacle leaves behind." Kayla turned the cloth over and rubbed his leg once again. Then she doused his leg again and tossed the towel into the bucket. "Get me a hot pack." When Clark handed her one, she placed the pack against his leg.

"What was that?" Petey asked as he hurried over, kneeling next to him on the wet deck.

"Portuguese man-of-war. The darn things are pretty rare around here, but this is the season when they show up." Kayla kept the hot pack on the sting, and the pain lessened.

Everyone else was on board, and they pulled up the anchor. Tommy helped Grayson back to a seat, and he put his leg up. The damn thing throbbed, so he continued using the hot pack. Petey got him some juice as they rode back to the resort, then sat next to him as Grayson drank his juice, leg thumping nervously. Tommy fussed over him, bringing him something to eat.

Grayson wasn't hungry and his stomach felt tetchy and upset. He asked for some water and closed his eyes, trying to will away the pain. He'd been hurt before, breaking his arm as a kid and spraining his ankle, but none of that compared to this. He breathed deeply and drank some more water. "Go have something to eat and some juice," he told Petey, holding Tommy's hand.

"Are you really okay?" Tommy squeezed gently.

"I'll be fine." Grayson gritted his teeth once again. The damn thing ached like a son of a bitch.

"The stings are often really painful, but it will get better in a few hours. They don't usually last too long," Kayla said as she lifted the hot pack and set it on the seat. "Don't keep this on too long."

"It looks like I've been...."

"Whipped. That's typical." Kayla handed him a fresh towel and gently put it over the stung area. "One got me last year. They hurt for a while and then the venom disperses. The wound should be gone in a few days. Just keep it clean and wait it out."

Grayson wasn't happy with the answer, but at least he wasn't going to die or anything. "Do you get these very often?"

"No. This time of year, the wind is right and they blow in from the Atlantic. Luckily we don't have a long man-o-war season here." She took one more look at his leg. "We'll be at the dock in a little while. Take it easy and let me know if it gets worse."

Grayson nodded.

"Don't worry. We'll keep a watch on him," Tommy said, and Grayson saw him and Petey share a look. Grayson doubted he was going anywhere without his two mother hens for a while.

When they arrived at the dock, Grayson was the last to disembark. His leg ached something terrible, and each step only added to it. Thankfully they didn't have far to go. He kept quiet about it, trying to walk as normally as possible, heading back to the bungalow. By the time they arrived, he was tired and went right to the bedroom to lie down. Petey brought in a pan that smelled like window cleaner. Grayson washed his leg in the ammonia solution, as the tour staff had recommended. "Thank you." He lay back and closed his eyes.

"Your leg is swollen," Tommy said when he came in behind Petey.

"It's probably from the sting." Grayson kept his eyes closed. "They said the pain would go away in a few hours, so I'm going to lie here and wait it out." He only wanted to go to sleep, and whatever kind of venom this stuff was, it seemed to make him sleepy. Maybe that was a good thing. He could rest, and when he woke again, he'd feel better. That was probably the best he could hope for. A burning sensation raced up his leg, but he tried to keep it out of his expression. He didn't want Tommy and Petey to worry. It would be over soon.

"Do you want something to drink?" Petey asked.

"No. Just let me rest for a while." There was nothing anyone could do but wait it out, and he wasn't going to make everyone else's day miserable. Peace and quiet would be the best thing for him. "Go play some video games and come tell me who wins."

Tommy and Petey lingered but eventually left the room, keeping the door partially open.

God, Grayson felt like he'd run a long race and just needed to rest and breathe. Then he felt more and more tired, so he closed his eyes and let go.

Chapter Nine

TOMMY left Grayson's room while Petey got the video game set up. They played a round, and then he went in to check on Grayson. He had closed his eyes and seemed to be resting, so he left him alone, returning to the game.

Petey beat him once again, mostly because he was worried about Grayson. Tommy went into the bedroom and saw Grayson had rolled onto his side. The room was a little warm, but not hot. He approached Grayson and touched his forehead, pulling his hand back right away. Grayson was burning up. His leg was even more swollen, and Grayson's breathing seemed forced and labored.

Tommy picked up the phone next to the bed and dialed the resort operator.

"Front desk, how may I help you?"

"We need some medical help. Grayson was stung by a man-of-war, and I think he's having an allergic reaction. We need help right away. Get an ambulance." At home, Tommy would have dialed 911, but here, he wasn't sure that was correct. "We need help now. His breathing is ragged, and I don't know how bad he's going to get. Please get help fast."

"Hang on." She set down the phone, and he heard her making another call. She spoke rapidly in the local language, then came back on the line. "They are sending an ambulance right away."

"Thank you." Tommy hung up as Petey came in the room, as white as a sheet.

"Daddy," he said, hurrying to the bed. "Wake up."

Tommy knew he had to be calm. Petey needed something to do. "Can you go to the bathroom and wet a cloth with cold water?"

Petey raced to the bathroom, and Tommy sat with Grayson, feeling completely helpless. He kept listening for a siren, but heard nothing but the lap of the waves. His nervousness increased by the second. Petey returned with the cloth, and Tommy wiped Grayson's forehead, then placed the cloth on it to try to help with the fever.

"Is he going to be okay?" Petey asked, near tears.

Tommy took his hand, squeezed it, and nodded. It was all he was able to do. Words weren't going to come.

Finally the two-toned European-type siren could be heard getting closer.

"Stay here with him." Tommy patted the edge of the bed, and Petey sat down while Tommy hurried out to the door, pulled it open, and directed the ambulance men inside. He followed them and took Petey by the hand, tugging him gently from the room.

"They need to be able to get to him," Tommy told him gently, Petey pulled on his hand to try to get free.

"Daddy," Petey cried, sounding like a child, but that was okay. Fear did that.

"He's going to be okay. They're here to help him."

"What happened?" one of the men asked.

Tommy answered, hugging Petey. "We were snorkeling and he was stung by a Portuguese something. That was a few hours ago. Do you think this is a reaction to that?"

"Probably," the man answered, turning back to Grayson. Another man came in with a gurney, and they loaded Grayson on it. "We're going to transport him to the hospital. We believe he's having an allergic reaction to the venom."

Tommy bit his lower lip as he watched them lift Grayson. One of the men had a breathing mask over Grayson's mouth and nose and was using a bulb, probably to help him breathe.

Petey clung to him, and Tommy wasn't sure what to do as they wheeled Grayson out of the bungalow.

"Can't we go too?"

"There isn't going to be room." Tommy closed up the bungalow and guided Petey out after the gurney. A taxi waited near the entrance of the resort, so Tommy hailed it. He and Petey got in back. "Follow the ambulance. We need to get to the hospital."

The driver nodded and pulled out when they did, though the ambulance sped through the limited traffic. Tommy chewed his nails, still holding Petey as he did his best to keep it in sight. The drive was only a few minutes, and they pulled up to the small hospital. After Tommy paid the fare, they got out and hurried inside, where he tried to explain why he was there and what was going on.

"It's all right," a lady of about fifty or so, dressed in white, with a heavy Caribbean accent, explained. "He's in back and being seen by a doctor now." She pointed to some plastic chairs. "Please sit down, and I'll see when you can go back."

Tommy nodded and moved to the chair, Petey clinging to him out of sheer fear.

"What if…," Petey croaked, and Tommy gently rubbed his head. He didn't have any answers, so all he could do was comfort Petey as best he could, while his own fears surfaced and threatened to run away with him. He had to keep it together for Petey's sake.

Tommy sat with Petey next to him, watching the door like a hawk. "He's strong and healthy. Your dad is going to be okay." God, he wasn't sure if he was trying to reassure Petey or himself. Grayson certainly hadn't looked okay when they'd wheeled him out of the bungalow. He had groaned, but he was pale, and Tommy hated the fact that they seemed to have to help him breathe. That certainly wasn't a good sign.

Tommy put an arm around Petey's shoulders to try to reassure him, but he wasn't sure how successful he was. He hated just sitting there waiting. There were few things that made him feel more helpless.

Petey's right leg bounced up and down on the floor, sending a vibration through the chairs. He gasped and held his breath as the door opened, then nudged Tommy, who lifted his gaze as a tall blond doctor, judging by the coat he was wearing, headed across the packed waiting area to them.

"Are you with Mr. Phillips?"

"Yes. This is Petey, his son, and I'm his boyfriend, Tommy Gordon. We're all here on vacation together."

"Is my dad going to be okay?" Petey asked, jumping to his feet. He looked about two seconds from making a dash back toward that door to try to find Grayson. Not that Tommy blamed him.

The doctor knelt down in front of Petey. "We're doing the best we can for him. I promise," he said with a slight European accent.

Petey nodded and sat back down, and Tommy followed the doctor a few steps away.

"He's had a violent allergic reaction to the venom. We've given him something to counteract it, as well as to try to reverse some of the effects of his reaction, but it's going to take some time. He's stable right now, but his airway was nearly completely blocked by the time he got here."

"Oh God." Tommy willed his legs not to give out. He had just realized how much Grayson meant to him and he wasn't going to lose him so soon. He couldn't, and neither could Petey.

"As I said, he is stable at the moment, and we've been able to insert a breathing tube so he is getting oxygen. We'll continue to try giving him antihistamines in order to lessen the swelling that seems to be happening all through his body. We are doing everything we can right now, but all we can do is wait to see if he responds the way we hope he will."

Tommy nodded rather blankly. This was like being punched in the stomach. "Can we see him?"

The doctor paused. "I don't advise it right now. His face and body are swollen and puffy. Hopefully in the next few hours that will begin to go down as the medication takes effect. Please just wait and be patient. If anything further happens, I will have someone let you know. But the best thing for him right now is rest."

"Is he conscious?"

"No. He has muttered for Petey and Tommy, and I'm assuming that's the two of you. He isn't in a coma or completely unconscious." The doctor turned toward the door. "I'll let you know as soon as I can." He hurried away, and Tommy sat beside Petey again, explaining what he could and then settling in to wait and pray. Tommy held on to Grayson's strength and health as hard as he could. It was all he had to keep him going.

"He's going to be okay," he told Petey for what seemed like the millionth time, and continued holding him, knowing his first job for Grayson was to make sure Petey was taken care of. "Are you hungry?"

Petey nodded, and Tommy got up with him to go looking for something to eat. They found a small stand with some coffee, drinks, and a few sandwiches and things. He bought what Petey wanted and let him eat, wishing he had some sort of appetite. But he was too upset and worried to eat. They returned to the waiting room and sat down once again for what felt like hours as other people in the area came and went.

"Mr. Gordon," the nurse said as she approached. Tommy stood, nervous as hell. "Dr. Krause asked me to bring you back." She waited for them to follow, and Tommy guided Petey with him through the hallways and down a white corridor to a small room. Grayson lay on the bed, eyes closed, looking pale as ever. "He's breathing on his own now, and a lot of the swelling has gone down."

Tommy said a silent prayer. Grayson was still somewhat puffy, but apparently whatever they had given him was working.

"Dad," Petey said as he walked to the side of the bed and took Grayson's hand. "Please wake up."

"He's still out from all the medication he's been given," the nurse explained in a soft Caribbean accent that seemed so soothing to Tommy's jangled nerves.

Tommy took a place near Petey, an arm protectively around his shoulders. "He's going to be okay. The swelling is better, and they said he's sleeping because of all of the medication." He pointed to the IV on the stand on the other side of the bed. Tommy hadn't given much thought to the kind of facilities they might have on the island, but Bonaire was Dutch, so it figured it would be part of their medical system. "I bet he can hear you, though. So if you want to tell him something, I'm sure it's okay," Tommy whispered to Petey, then stepped back to give him a few minutes of privacy with him.

"Daddy," Petey said softly, wiping the tears from his eyes. "You gotta get better. If you do, I promise to be good and to listen to you all the time. I'll even let you win at video games." He sniffled, and Tommy smiled a little. Grayson was awful at them, so that was a real sacrifice. "Please, Dad, you just gotta get better. I'm really scared."

Tommy came forward once again. "He's been very brave, Grayson, we both have, but you're scaring us." He took Grayson's hand from Petey, who sat in the chair next to the bed, staring at the far wall, his foot bouncing once again. Tommy leaned over the bed. "Grayson, you need to open your eyes and talk to us." He waited, and Grayson's eyes fluttered but stayed closed. "I love you, Grayson, and I want to see where things go between us. I want both you and Petey in my life. I want to make you happy for the rest of your life. You need to get better and come back to us. Petey and I both need you very much." He gently rubbed Grayson's hand with his thumb.

"Tommy?" Grayson croaked, and Petey hurried over.

"Dad!" he cried, and Grayson let go of his hand to take Petey's.

Carefully, he turned his head. "I heard you, son. I heard both of you." He breathed deeply and his eyes fluttered open. "Are you both okay?"

"Just scared," Petey said. "Uncle Tommy stayed with me and got me something to eat. But I was so scared, and they wouldn't let us see you for a long time." He leaned closer, and Grayson patted Petey's head.

"It's okay, son. I'm feeling better now, and things don't hurt like they did." He smiled, and Petey leaned over the bed, his head resting on Grayson's shoulder, Petey crying softly. "Don't cry. I'm going to be fine."

Tommy blinked his own tears from his eyes, wiping them with the back of his hand. "You had us both really scared."

"I know, and I'm sorry." Grayson took Tommy's hand as Petey lay partially on him, holding him. "I didn't mean to scare either of you. I guess I had a reaction to the venom."

"Yeah. It was bad, and they said you were all puffy and that you couldn't breathe." Petey babbled on, and Grayson comforted him, his gorgeous eyes locking with Tommy's.

"Did you mean what you said?"

Tommy nodded. "I'm not afraid anymore. Whatever happens when we get home, I want you in my life—both of you. The only thing I'm afraid of is losing you." He wiped his eyes once again and let Grayson comfort Petey.

"How long do you have to stay here?" Petey asked.

"I don't know. But I'm going to be okay now." He held Petey, and Tommy slowly stepped around the IV stand to stroke Grayson's arm.

"You're doing better, I see," the nurse said as she came in, and Tommy moved out of the way. "How do you feel?"

"Like my body is too big for my skin." Grayson was trying to be funny, but it wasn't working.

"The swelling is going down, and you're looking better than you were an hour ago." She checked him over and glanced at the IV. "I'll tell the doctor so he can come in and look you over. But you're doing a lot better." She checked Grayson's blankets and left the room.

"Tommy," Grayson whispered. "I'm going to need you to get me some clothes. I think they cut what I had off me. At least I sort of remember that."

"I'll go back and get what you need." Tommy moved closer again and stroked Grayson's arm. "How much do you remember about what happened?"

"Just snippets, I guess." Grayson's eyes drooped and his voice became softer. "But I remember what you said, and you can't take it back." He closed his eyes, and Petey grew agitated.

"He's only sleeping, which is what he needs." Tommy walked around the bed to put his arm around Petey. "He's coming out of it and getting better now." He swallowed hard, realizing just how close they'd come to losing him. If he hadn't checked on Grayson when he had, he might have been unable to breathe and could have died in the bungalow. They'd all been very lucky. "Stay here with your dad and don't leave the room. Hold his hand and talk to him. I'm going to see if I can find someone to see what's going on."

"That won't be necessary," Dr. Krause said as he strode into the room. "He's responding well to the medication, and I suspect he's going to be fine now. We're going to keep him here for a few more hours so the swelling and effects of the toxin clear out of his system, and then he can go back to the resort. He'll need some medication for a few days and plenty of rest."

"He'll get that." If Tommy had to tie Grayson to the bed, he'd make sure he rested. "We're supposed to travel soon."

"I suspect he'll be fine. Just don't let him overdo it." Dr. Krause checked Grayson over, waking him to look into his eyes, and then backed away once again. "Give him a few hours."

"Okay. Petey and I are going to go back to the resort and will bring him some clothes. I also want to get Petey a proper dinner. Can someone call us when he's ready to be released?" Tommy gave the doctor his number, and then he and Petey said goodbye to Grayson, promising they'd be back as soon as they could.

Tommy escorted Petey out of the hospital after explaining that he couldn't stay here with his dad alone. They called a taxi for the ride back to the resort, and Tommy got the bag they used for their outings and packed some of Grayson's clothes. Once that was done, he took Petey to the restaurant by the pool and let Petey get something to eat. Tommy's appetite was returning and he ate a little, relieved that Grayson was going to be okay.

"You said you loved my dad," Petey said as he shoveled french fries into his mouth.

"I do. I love your dad, and I think he loves me too. Is that okay?" Tommy asked, hoping Petey would give them his blessing.

"Dad asked me the same thing," Petey said. "Why?"

Tommy sighed. "Because you're important to both of us. Your dad and I want to be happy, but we want you happy too." He stole a fry from Petey, offering him some of his salad in return.

"I love my dad too."

"I know you do, and I know you'd do anything he wanted you to. That's why we both asked to make sure we know what you want."

Petey ate another fry and smiled. "I like you too. You are always nice to me, and you don't do things behind my dad's back the way Jeffrey did. He used to be mean sometimes when Dad wasn't looking and then tell Dad that I was misbehaving. Then Dad would send me to my room. I finally told Dad about it and he believed me, though, and he talked to Jeffrey and he didn't do that anymore." Petey grinned. "Dad always believes me, even about stuff at school."

Tommy chuckled. "That's because Grayson is a good dad and you tell the truth. If you always do that, even if it's bad, then people will believe you. That's how it works. So I don't lie to you and you don't lie to me. I'll tell you that I love your dad and that he's important to me, and you're important to me too. That's the truth."

Petey nodded and slipped off his chair. He put his arms around Tommy, and Tommy returned the hug. "I love you too."

Tommy closed his eyes, swallowing hard as he digested what Petey had just told him. He'd not only been given the seal of approval, but Petey loved him. Two people in one week had told him that he was loved. That had to be a record, and the heart Xavier had broken seemed to be knitting itself back together more strongly than ever.

They finished their dinner, and Tommy got them a taxi back to the hospital. When they got back to see Grayson, he looked much better, sitting up and drinking some water and juice. Tommy gave him the clothes, and Grayson held the bag on his lap.

"How are you?"

"The doctor says I'm doing very well. They drew some blood and were going to check something, and then they said if it looked good, I'd be ready to go." Grayson sat on the edge of the bed, and Tommy pulled the curtain so he could get dressed with a little privacy.

"You really seem better." Tommy smiled, and once Grayson had his pants on, Petey came around to sit next to him.

"I'm glad you're okay, Dad."

Grayson hugged him close. "Me too. I'm sorry if I scared you." He sat back on the bed. "I'm going to be tired for a while. The doctor said that I've been through a lot and can expect to sleep pretty much the next few days."

"Tomorrow you can rest all you want, and the day after you can sit on planes and in the airports. We'll even get you one of those carts that beeps." Tommy would do anything to keep Grayson comfortable and not let him exert himself.

"I think I'm ready to go home." Grayson closed his eyes. Tommy had to agree with him—he was ready to go too. After all, he had what he really wanted… more than he'd ever thought possible when he came here.

GRAYSON was released a little while later, and Tommy and Petey took him back to the resort and got him settled in the king-sized bed. Tommy set out a buffet of junk food and let Petey go at it. They both needed something to take their minds off the catastrophe that they'd averted. Stuffed to the gills, Petey went to bed a little while later after spending some time alone with his dad.

Once the bungalow was quiet, Tommy wandered out onto the dock and sat cross-legged, looking out at the stars. "What is it about this place?" he whispered under his breath, closing his eyes and letting the lap of waves and the soft clang of bells, as well as the creak of a nearby dock as it moved in the surf, settle deep into his essence. This was what he wanted, the peace he'd searched for. His head usually swam with overlapping ideas and worries, never letting up, but right now his head was still, at peace.

"I hope it's because you're relaxed and content for the first time in months," Grayson said from behind him.

"Can you read my mind?" Tommy asked.

"I know you, remember? You spend so much of your time restless because your head never lets you settle." Grayson shuffled closer and sat down beside him.

"I know. But it's settled now. It took all week, and now I feel like I'm away on vacation." He turned around as he thought things over. "But I don't think that's it, because I've been on vacation before."

"Did you ever think that it's because you're happy? That you're allowed to be truly, bone-deep happy?" Grayson slipped his arms around him. "You finally let go."

Tommy humphed. "Maybe I'm simply worn out after everything." He ran his hands over Grayson's arms, the hair tickling his palms. "But yes, I'm happy."

Grayson chuckled. "It took you long enough to admit it."

"You should go back to bed." Tommy turned slowly to face Grayson. "You got out of the hospital a few hours ago. You need to rest and get your strength up. And no more time in the water for you." After all this, Tommy had probably had more than enough of water sports for this trip.

"I will. I've been lying down a lot and thought I'd see where you were." Grayson got to his feet with a soft groan. "Getting older sucks."

"You'll be okay. The stiffness is probably a residual reaction from the sting." Tommy stood as well and helped Grayson back inside, closing the sliding door. He sent Grayson to his room and checked on Petey, who was sound asleep, curled up on his side. When he returned to the bedroom, Grayson was in bed once more, eyes closed, already on his way to dreamland. Tommy cleaned up quietly, then climbed under the sheets. Grayson scooted closer, and Tommy held him, his hands sliding over his warm belly.

"I love you, Tommy, and that isn't going to change," Grayson mumbled, rolling over. "So stop worrying about stuff and just go to sleep. Everything is going to work out."

"How do you know?" Tommy asked, and Grayson tugged him closer.

Grayson mumbled something, then cleared his throat. "That's easy. What do you want more than anything?"

"You and Petey in my life, with me, forever. I love you with everything I have." A slice of fear ran up him, but it dissipated quickly.

"And I love you. I have for a long time. It's that simple. I want you in my life, and we'll work out the rest." Grayson shifted gently on the mattress and then chuckled. "But you know we did do things a little backward." His voice was already slurring a little as he slipped into sleep.

Tommy stilled. "Huh?" He barely understood what Grayson was saying.

Grayson tugged him closer. "We had the honeymoon first."

Epilogue

A Year Later

"HI, Pop," Petey said, dropping his backpack on the heavy oak bench near the front door as he zoomed into the house. Tommy smiled at the name. It had appeared in Petey's speech just a few weeks before, and it tickled him no end every time he heard it. "Are we ready to go?" He barely stopped as he made his way to the kitchen.

"I put out a snack for you, and your dad will be home in half an hour. When you're done eating, you can help me load the car, and then we'll be off as soon as he gets home." Tommy brought the last bag down and set it by the door. "Are there any last-minute things you need?" He and Petey had already gone over the list, and Grayson had helped him pack.

"I think I'm good." The stool scraped the floor, and Tommy smiled, knowing Petey was sitting at the snack bar. He was growing like a weed and had to have shot up six inches in the last year, looking more and more like his handsome father every day. Tommy checked that he had all the bags, counting them twice, and then went to his office to log in to make sure all his updates had been made. He also called his assistant, Ted, letting him know how to get in touch with him. The addition of Ted to his life had been Grayson's suggestion, and he was a godsend. Reliable and trustworthy, he took care of a lot of the mundane details so Tommy could do what he did best. The overall work-related stress in his life had diminished significantly because he no longer had to try to remember every detail.

"We're leaving, and I'll be back in a little over a week," Tommy told him.

"Your calendar is cleared, and we'll be ready for full-scale launch when you get back. Just relax and have a good time." Ted paused on the line. "I made all those arrangements you asked for, and I'm texting them to you now. I wish to heck I was going on this trip. It sounds awesome, and I know you'll have a great time."

"Call if you need anything," Tommy said as he heard a car in the driveway.

Ted gasped. "I will not. There are plenty of people here who can handle anything that comes up. You and Grayson have the time of your lives. You deserve it. Now, you better get going. You need to leave soon." Ted was almost more anal about things than Tommy was... almost.

"Okay." Tommy ended the call as Grayson came in the front door.

"Hey," he said softly, his smile radiant. Grayson set his case next to Petey's backpack, then strode across the oak-paneled entrance hall to sweep Tommy into his arms. "How does it feel to be an old married man?" Before Tommy could answer, Grayson kissed him, sending a wave of heat racing through him as Tommy went weak in the knees.

"I don't know. You're the old man." Tommy grinned before hugging Grayson tightly.

"Kid present," Petey called.

Grayson rolled his eyes. "You need to help load the car."

Petey came in and hurried to the front door, hauling luggage outside. "I'll help him—you make sure the house is closed up." They had decided to move into Tommy's home because both he and Grayson loved the architectural gem.

Tommy made sure all the windows and doors were locked, took care of the last dishes in the kitchen before checking that all the luggage was loaded, and then they climbed into Tommy's midnight blue BMW sedan and started the trip to Chicago. Grayson drove, and Tommy sat in the passenger seat, with Petey in back. They were on their way, excitement filling the car. Grayson reached over, and Tommy took his hand when they entered the freeway. This was perfection.

LATE the following afternoon, their small plane circled the larger island and then passed over the smaller one on its path into the airport. "This is going to be great," Grayson said. "And don't worry about anything. I have every allergy medication and emergency treatment known to man with me."

"There's the resort, Dad." Petey pointed down below as they drew closer to the ground, passing over the coast.

"Yup. We booked the same bungalow, and we're doing some of the same things that we did last year." Grayson grinned as Tommy squeezed his hand. Tommy hadn't been sure he wanted to return to Bonaire for their honeymoon, but Grayson had suggested it, and the more Tommy thought about it, the more he liked it.

"But no one is getting stung this time," Tommy chastised both of them, and Petey and Grayson saluted and then broke into fits of giggles.

"Sweetheart, it's okay. Everything is going to be great. We've done this before." Grayson grinned.

"That's what I'm worried about." Tommy wrung his hands slightly.

"Come on. Think about everything we got out of that trip. It truly was the best worst honeymoon ever."

Tommy chuckled. He had gotten a lot—hell, everything that had become important to him—out of that trip. "If that's true, then what's this trip going to be?"

"The best best honeymoon ever," Petey answered, and Tommy smiled, leaning closer to Grayson, who kissed him just as the wheels of the plane touched the ground.

Coming in July 2018

REAMSPUN DESIRES

Dreamspun Desires #61
Stranger in a Foreign Land by Michael Murphy

Losing his old life and finding a new love.

After an accident stole his memory, the only home American businessman Patrick knows is Bangkok. He recovers under the tender ministrations of Jack, an Australian ex-pat who works nights at a pineapple cannery. Together they search for clues to Patrick's identity, but without success. Soon that forgotten past seems less and less important as Jack and Patrick—now known as Buddy—build a new life together.

But the past comes crashing in when Patrick's brother travels to Thailand looking for him… and demands Patrick return to Los Angeles, away from Jack and the only world familiar to him. The attention also causes trouble for Jack, and to make their way back to each other, Patrick will need to find not only himself, but Jack as well, before everything is lost….

Dreamspun Desires #62
A Fool and His Manny by Amy Lane

Seeing the truth and falling in love.

Dustin Robbins-Grayson was a surly adolescent when Quinlan Gregory started the nanny gig. After a rocky start, he grew into Quinlan's friend and confidant—and a damned sexy man.

At twenty-one, Dusty sees how Quinlan sacrificed his own life and desires to care for Dusty's family. He's ready to claim Quinlan—he's never met a kinder, more capable, more lovable man. Or a lonelier one. Quinlan has spent his life as the stranger on the edge of the photograph, but Dusty wants Quinlan to be the center of his world. First he has to convince Quinlan he's an adult, their love is real, and Quinlan can be more than a friend and caregiver. Can he show Quin that he deserves to be both a man and a lover, and that in Dusty's eyes, he's never been "just the manny?"

Now Available

REAMSPUN DESIRES

Dreamspun Desires #57
Stand by Your Manny by Amy Lane
Learning to trust and falling in love.

Sammy Lowell has his hands full juggling his music, college, some pesky health problems, and making the uncles who raised him proud. He needs help fulfilling his after-school duties with his siblings. Nobody can be in two places at once—not even Sammy!

An injury puts Cooper Hoskins in a tough spot—if he can't work, the foster sister he's raising can't eat. But years in the foster system have left Cooper short on trust, and opening up to accept help isn't easy.

Luckily, family intervenes—Cooper needs a job so he can care for Felicity, and Sammy needs someone who can see past his illness to the wonderful things he has planned for his life. Each heals the damaged places in the other's heart. But falling in love is a big responsibility for young men deep in family already. Can the two of them get past their fear of the immediate future to see forever with each other?

Dreamspun Desires #58
Bad to the Bone by Nicki Bennett
A second chance at first love—if he has the courage to take it.

Alex can't think of himself as anything but a failure. In high school, he was on the fast track to a career in pro football when he forged an unlikely friendship with a half-Comanche boy from the wrong part of town, Ricky Lee Jennings. Their shared love of books could have grown into more—but a homophobic teammate attacked Ricky Lee, and Alex wouldn't risk his scholarship to defend him. Ricky Lee was kicked out of school, and Alex never heard from him again.

Now Alex's glory days are nothing but a memory. An injury ended his football aspirations, his marriage fell apart, and his dreams of making a difference as an environmental lobbyist are as dead as his fantasies of sports stardom.

But all that could change in one magical night, when Ricky Lee shows up at their high school reunion.

SARASOTA FINE DINING

Restaurant Name	Address	Phone #
Euphemia Haye	5540 Gulf of Mexico Dr	383-3633
Harry's Continental Kit.	525 St Judes Dr	383-0777
Louies Modern	1289 N Palm Ave	552-9688
Maison Blanche	2605 Gulf of Mexico Dr	383-8088
Michael's On East	1212 East Ave	366-0007
Mozaic	1377 Main St	951-6272
Ophelia's on the Bay	9105 Midnight Pass	349-2212
Pattigeorge's	7120 Gulf of Mexico Dr	383-5111
Pier 22	1200 1st Avenue W	748-8087
Pomona Bistro	481 N Orange Ave	706-1677
Roast Restaurant & Bar	1296 First St	953-1971

UPSCALE CHAIN DINING

Restaurant Name	Address	Phone #
Bonefish Grill	3971 S Tamiami Trl	924-9090
Bonefish Grill	8101 Cooper Crk Blvd	360-3171
Brio Tuscan Grille	190 Univ. Town Ctr Dr	702-9102
The Capital Grille	180 Univ. Town Ctr Dr	256-3647
Carrabba's Italian Grill	1940 Stickney Pt Rd	925-7407
Carrabba's Italian Grill	5425 University Pkwy	355-4116
Cheesecake Factory	130 Univ. Town Ctr Dr	256-3760
First Watch	1395 Main St	954-1395
Kona Grill	150 Univ. Town Ctr Dr	256-8005
Lee Roy Selmons	8253 Cooper Crk Blvd	360-3287
P.F. Changs	766 S Osprey Ave	296-6002
Seasons 52	170 Univ. Town Ctr Dr	702-9652